THE ODDS WERE RIGHT FOR VICTORY

The problem with computer warfare is that the computer is always logical while the human enemy is not— or doesn't have to be.

And that's what the Betastani enemy were doing— nothing that the Alphaland computers said they would. Those treacherous foemen were avoiding logic and using such unheard-of devices as surprise and sabotage, treason and trickery. They even had Alphaland's Deputy of Information believing Betastani propaganda without even realizing it.

Of course he still thought he was being loyal to Alphaland, because he thought that one and one must logically add up to two. And that kind of thinking could make him the biggest traitor of them all.

MACK REYNOLDS

World traveler, expert observer of the human condition, a favorite science-fiction writer for more than two decades, Mack Reynolds makes his home in a small town in Mexico. He is the author of more than two hundred sf short stories, novelettes and novels, many of which have been published by Ace Books.

COMPUTER WAR

by

MACK REYNOLDS

WILDSIDE PRESS

COMPUTER WAR

PART ONE

I

NUMBER ONE SAID, "Coaids, we are in session."

The murmuring dropped away to be replaced by respectful silence.

With the others, Ross Westley gave full attention to his ultimate leader. He had read somewhere that eventually a person's character was reflected in his face. Were it true, then Number One was overly fond of the sensual pleasures as well as power. As a young man, he must have been exceptionally handsome; now, at approximately seventy, his face had gone gross, his smile, when it did appear, humorless. His voice, even when addressing these, his closest associates, was empty of inflection save that of command.

It was said, Ross knew, that since the cruelly suppressed revolt of Maximilian Barker, for years Number Two in the Alphaland hierarchy, the Presidor had only one intimate. His vices, did they exist, and his face proclaimed they existed, were enjoyed in solitude. It was said he was a connoisseur of vintages, in spite of the United Temple's ban on alcoholic beverages, and a gourmet with a staff of half the best chefs on the planet. It was even said he took tobacco, in some form or other.

Number One said now, "Coaid Graves."

Graves was not a member of the Central Comita and nervously shuffled his papers in this august gathering.

He said, "The computers reveal that Betastan could be reduced with a short, sharp conflict lasting 2.35 months, plus or minus 3.8 days. The cost in casualties would be 17,900 killed and 310,000 wounded, plus or minus 293 killed and 7,021 wounded. The cost would be

127,895,367,400 gold Alphas, plus or minus 6,730,412."

Number One looked at his Deputy of Finance, who indicated unhappiness.

"Coaid Matheison?"

Deputy Matheison jiggled a stylo. He was obviously in awe of his leader and his voice came in apology. "It seems fantastically expensive for a war lasting two months. Your Leadership is familiar with the state of the treasury."

Marshal of the Armies Rupert Croft-Gordon, without being called upon, said heavily, "The more mechanized modern warfare becomes, the more expensive. Firepower increases geometrically every decade, but so does the cost of keeping a man in the field."

Number One looked at him. He said, "We shall hear from you shortly, Marshal Croft-Gordon."

The Marshal flushed.

Number One said, "Coaid Wilkonson, what does our geopolitician think of the project?"

The nattily goateed Wilkonson was at home in any gathering, from undergraduate students to the highest echelons of the government of his land.

"The Presidor is already cognizant of the situation. Our planet is divided into two major land areas and two major powers, Alphaland and Betastan, and twenty-three minor powers. Geographically, we almost duplicate each other, and, as all know, down through history this has led to neither one being able to dominate the smaller nations. There has been too delicate a balance. If Alphaland were able to bring its rival to its knees, then the world government which Your Leadership foresees would become an immediate reality. It is doubtful that even a confederation of the minor powers could stand before our glorious march."

Temple Bishop Stockwater murmured unctuously, "Amen."

Ross Westley, conscious of his comparative youth,

6

seldom spoke at these gatherings. Now he shifted in his chair.

Number One looked at him. "And our Deputy of Propaganda?"

Ross said unhappily, looking at the last speaker, and then over at the computer expert, "The figures deal with a quick war between Alphaland and Betastan. What would happen if some of the neutrals, seeing the handwriting on the wall, entered on the side of the enemy?"

"Well, Coaid?" Number One said to Graves.

Graves shuffled his papers again. "Of the twenty-three, the computers reveal that only twelve could mobilize in time to affect the conflict. Of these twelve, the computers report that four would favor our cause, four favor that of Betastan, and four remain neutral. None of these twelve are strong neutral powers. If the Presidor would like more details . . ."

"Not now."

Number One sat and thought. It was a long-time habit of his. Not a sound came from his associates. The story was that almost twenty years ago a deputy had gone into a coughing spasm during one of the Presidor's retreats into contemplation and had never again attended a command session, losing his office within a matter of weeks.

He said finally, "And our Academecian of Socioeconomics?"

Academecian Philip McGivern was a very old man, his beard almost identical to that of Wilkonson but a dirty gray rather than black.

He stood to speak, although none of the others had. McGivern was an Old Hand and bore no awe for Number One—they had been through too much together. He looked full into the face of the other and said, "You are acquainted with my opinions, Your Leadership. I assume you merely wish me to fill them in for these, our Coaids. We have reached the crisis that I warned about

7

a full ten years ago. The age of the computer is upon us. Ultimate automation. Our productive capacity alone is sufficient to supply the whole planet with manufactured goods. Our own land is glutted with them and industry is slowing, sometimes shutting down. As our commodities become increasingly cheaper, tariff walls are erected abroad to support the more expensive products of homeland industries. A full sixteen minor countries have all but completely forbidden imports from Alphaland.

"If the present socioeconomic system of Alphaland is to continue, we must have both foreign markets and sources of raw materials. If this war is successful, and world government achieved, our only policy can be one of reducing the economies of Betastan and all the neutral lands to pastoral societies. In the future, they can supply agricultural and mineral needs; we must supply all industrial production."

The old man finished significantly. "Otherwise, we shall have an industrial collapse within three months, plus or minus 3.2 days." His eyes turned to Graves. "According to my own computers."

Ross Westley stirred in his seat again.

Number One looked at him bleakly. "You seem restive, Coaid."

Ross nodded. "Your Leadership, I know my position isn't usually involved in the preliminary planning stages; however, that is going to have to be sold not only to the rest of the world, except Betastan, but to our own people as well. In spite of the computers predicting an easy victory, those over 300,000 casualties are going to be real people, our citizens. The civil war hasn't been over so long but that the people are horrified at the idea of more war. And to sell them a war of aggression at this stage . . ."

Number One interrupted. "My people will go where I lead them."

"Yes"—Ross nodded unhappily—"but it will not be a

8

simple task for those of us who have to point out the path."

Number One slumped back into thought.

Afterwards Ross Westley took a pneumatic back to his official quarters. He moved less than briskly through the outer offices, desks and office machines that composed the inner circles of the Commissariat of Information.

His staff, knowing his mood, didn't intrude, but near his own office he was brought up, his usual way being barred by a gleaming new computer of exotic design. Ross Westley stopped and glared at it.

He snapped at one of the senior secretaries, "What in the name of the Holy Ultimate is this?"

She looked mildly shocked at his language, and inadvertently shot a look over her shoulder but then caught herself in the realization that there would be no Temple Monks in the preserves of the Deputy of Propaganda. However, Jet Pirincin sometimes doubted that her chief was as devout as his high position would call for.

Jet said, apologetically, "The technicians are still installing it, Coaid Deputy."

"I said, what the hell is it? It's at the point where I can't get to my own office through the curd this place is littered with."

"Yes, Coaid Deputy Westley," Jet said. She was mildly surprised. Ross Westley was usually on the easygoing side, as upper echelon coaids went. "As I understand, sir, it is a new development adapted to our commissariat which, by scanning any printed page, can give a plus or minus percentage of two, on the effect of the publication on the public."

He looked at her sourly. "What's new about that, Coaid Pirincin? We've got a bank of machines that'll handle that sort of jetsam."

"Yes, Coaid Deputy. I wouldn't know, Coaid. The technicians know all about it. It's some new departure."

9

Ross snorted and sidestepped the new equipment to continue to his office. He muttered, "Why not turn the whole nardy government over to these technicians? They're the only ones who know what's going on."

Jet Pirincin stared after him, more than mildly surprised now. Suppose there had been a Surety Coaid about. Admittedly, Deputy Westley was a member of the Central Comita, though a junior one, but you simply didn't say such things. It amounted to criticism of the workings of the government. She shook her head. It was her opinion that Ross Westley was a pleasant enough boss to have, and even almost handsome in a craggy sort of way, but she decided it was just as well that his early training to be a teacher of history was thwarted. What might he have taught his students?

Ross growled at the door which opened automatically before him. It had been a long-time irritation. The damned mechanism didn't read his *mind*, it read his physical presence. Suppose his desire was to approach the door but not go through it. Suppose his desire was to come up to the door and press his ear against it, so as to eavesdrop on someone within. The damned door wouldn't let him! It opened, willy-nilly, upon his coming in proximity.

He grunted. sourly. At least it was an improvement over the doors of his youth. They couldn't read individuals and opened on the approach of anyone at all!

He realized he was in a miserable mood. He didn't like the developments of the Central Comita session this afternoon. He didn't like them at all. To the extent possible, he had been fighting the trend, but the Deputy of Propaganda was a low man on the totem pole and often not even called on to attend inmost staff sessions.

He sat and stared moodily and unseeingly at his orderbox. Finally he flicked a finger to activate it and said, "Is there anything on my desk?"

A voice answered him in detail and he said, "Switch

it to Assistant Deputy Bauserman and cut all calls to me for the next two hours."

"Yes, Coaid."

He sat for a moment, then surreptitiously flicked a small stud on the ring on his right little finger, with the thumbnail of his left hand. From the side of his eyes, he observed what would seem to be a star sapphire set in the ring. It gleamed no more than ordinarily.

Evidently, he decided, his complaint of a month or so ago had brought results. If the highly developed little mop he had in the ring was effective, his quarters were no longer bugged. Rank had its privileges, even in the Free Democratic Commonwealth of Alphaland.

He got to his feet, went over to what would appear to be a closet door and opened it. The personal pneumatic car inside was strictly a one-man affair. He wedged into it, closed the door behind him, threw the vacuum control, and began dialing his destination. He was too orientated to the transportation method to be distressed by the sudden drop-away and then the surge of acceleration.

The car came to a halt and flicked the green light for him. He threw off the vacuum control, opened the door and stepped out. He was at the entry port of one of Alphacity's more popular parks. He considered momentarily, but then threw the control which would send his car to a nearby parking area. His station would have allowed him to monopolize the place indefinitely but of recent months Ross Westley was, possibly unbeknownst to himself, becoming unhappy about many of his prerogatives.

He walked toward the park center, as though heading for the famed Interplanetary Zoo, but managed to check, two or three times over, whether or not he was being tailed. As far as he could see, he wasn't.

He started for his true destination.

11

Tilly Trice looked up at his entrance into her shop. She winked perkily and blew him a kiss, but didn't get up from her work.

She was, he told himself all over again, the most unlikely young woman a powerful and wealthy governmental head could ever expect to make himself a fool over. She was tiny. Her figure could hardly have been less, being that of a teenage boy, rather than one of the current TriDi sex symbols. Her face was pert rather than pretty, not to speak of beautiful. Admittedly, her features were clean, her carriage soldier-straight, her voice a dream of gentility.

But by no stretch of the imagination would any historic period of man's evolution, whether on Mother Earth or out here in the stars, have pinned the label of glamour girl on Tilly Trice.

At best, she would have made the grade as the famed girl next door, a boy's best pal.

She was fiddling with some red leather and a pot of glue. And it came to him that it was probably real leather. He wondered where she'd imported it from. Holy Ultimate, from Earth? The space freight alone! But then, of course, Tilly Trice's customers were the most ultra-wealthy the planet provided and were not of Alphaland alone. In fact, she boasted clients in every nation of this world.

She said, that faint mockery in her voice, "Hi, Coaid."

"Don't call me that," he growled.

She went, "Tu, tu, tu. Nardy temper today."

"Don't swear," he growled. "It doesn't become a half-pint. It sounds incongruous, a four letter word coming out of your mouth."

"Nardy," she said righteously, "is a five letter word. I know some four letter ones. You want to hear them?"

"No. Number One held another session today. Graves had the final computer returns."

She dropped her light air. "Oh," she said.

12

"They were as bad as I told you they would be. Graves gives Betastan a little better than two months."

"Oh, he does!" she said tartly, her attitude suddenly that of a defiant child.

He eyed her unhappily. "Listen, Till, what do your own computers carry on this? You've had enough material turned over to you to program . . ."

She was shaking her head to silence him. She got up and approached one of the dusty bookshelves that lined the shop's walls. She stared unseeingly at a short row of German language first editions.

Tilly shook her head again. "I won't give you any jetsam, Rossie. We have a few computers in Betastan, but nothing like the number you have here. None of them have been directed toward the military. Even after my warnings came through."

"But why not!"

She looked at him. "I think it's a bit difficult to explain our way of thinking to someone with your background, Rossie. But let me use an example. Back in the very old days on Earth, when the nations were perpetually arming—do you remember their terminology? They were all expending the gigantic sums involved in *defense.* It was a gobbledygook term. Nobody ever spent money on *offense,* it was always defense. By the oldest traditions of our race, the oldest teachings, he who lives by the sword, dies by it. And over and over again it was seen that those nations which built large military machines sooner or later found occasion to use them. Sometimes because they were attacked, more often they found occasion to attack—by flimsy excuse, or otherwise."

"What are you driving at?"

She sighed. "We're trying a new theory in Betastan."

"It's doomed to failure, you cloddies! Why do you think I've been acting the traitor for these past months? It's not just Betastan. Don't you realize that if this war

13

is lost, the whole planet eventually comes under the domination of Number One?"

She raised her eyebrows at him. "The war isn't lost."

He gave up.

He looked about the small store in despair. Finally he said, "You know, Till, I've sometimes wondered how you manage to transmit the information I've been giving you. I've known you for five years. For two of these I've known you to be connected with Betastan espionage. For the past eight months I've been feeding you the innermost secrets of Number One's private sessions with his deputies and closest coaids."

She tinkled laughter, but he went on, his forehead wrinkled. "I've gone to the trouble of checking out some of the methods our Commissariat of Surety uses to intercept espionage messages, and they're elaborate far beyond my first conception. Why, Deputy Mark Fielder has more computers devoted to that problem alone than I have in my whole commissariat."

Tilly Trice wickedly said, "I shouldn't trust you with this, Rossie, since you're not very good at keeping secrets. However"—she reached down and picked up a card from her desk—"I just mail a postcard through your post office."

II

THE PRESIDOR of the Free Democratic Commonwealth of Alphaland—known as Number One throughout the hierarchy—relaxed once he had passed through the doors of his private chambers. Perhaps slumped would have been the better term.

He headed for the moderately large living room which was his true home, and for the bar which sat in the corner there.

"This early in the day?" a voice said gently.

Pater Riggin sat in a leather armchair near the fireplace. He had evidently turned the thermostat down to the point where a fire was desirable. It was, Number One thought wryly, perhaps his lifelong friend's sole indulgence, sitting before the embers of a primitive blaze.

He spoke from the bar, even as he poured a double shotglass of Metaxa, imported from far Earth. "I sometimes wonder at the advisability of my having given you a key to my rooms. Sooner or later, in one of your typically absentminded moments, you'll either lose it, or, in one of your more idealistic spells, you'll decide that the Presidor of Alphaland has at long last become redundant and hand the key over to one of my none too few political opponents."

The Temple Monk closed the age-flimsy book he had been reading, but held the place with his right forefinger.

He said mildly, "The first is an admitted possibility. But who would know, upon finding it, that the ultra-remote Number One . . ."

"Don't call me that, Rig."

". . . excuse me, utilized a device as anachronistic as a lock and key to protect himself? In the second case, I am not a believer in the theory that displacing a dictator ends dictatorship. It merely opens the way to a different dictator, who may well be worse than the one just, eh, liquidated."

Number One brought his glass back to the fire and slumped into the chair across from his friend. He swallowed a larger amount than was his wont, in a gulp.

"So," he said, "you think you'd might as well support me."

The Temple Monk shook his head and sighed, patting his rounded tummy. "Only insofar as I have always supported you, Jim."

Number One twisted his mouth. "Mark Fielder sent

me a report last week which revealed that out in the boonies the common man thinks of you as my alter ego. Sort of a Svengali. When something goes more than ordinarily wrong in Alphaland, that curd of a Temple Monk is behind it."

Softly, Pater Riggin said, "And what was our good Deputy of Surety's suggestion?"

"That we shoot you, of course, and satisfy the yokes. They evidently could use a bit of satisfying these days."

Number One finished his Greek brandy and set the glass on a low table. Instead of immediately sinking back into his chair, he took up a stogie from a humidor. He selected an ancient style match, struck it under the table top, and drew smoke into his mouth and nasal passages.

Pater Riggin had never quite become used to the other's vice. Somehow, it didn't seem the thing that one would do, even before one's closest friend. He looked half away, not noting his companion's cynical expression.

Even Pater Riggin, Number One suspected, in his secret heart desired the Presidor of the Free Democratic Commonwealth to be a literal, rather than a propaganda, perfect man. He wondered, on occasion, what would happen if at this point in life he took a younger woman in marriage. Would the ultimate reaction lead to his overthrow, in this hypocritical society? He doubted if more than one person in ten among the citizenry realized that he had been married in his early years and that his wife had died on the barricades that accompanied his coming to power. It had been a long time ago, a very long time ago. And now the people thought him a lifelong abstainer from sex, as from every mundane pleasure. Inwardly, he snorted.

"What was decided at the session today, Jim?" the Temple Monk asked.

The other's eyes narrowed infinitesimally. "How did

you know there was a session of the inmost staff, Rig? That's strictly surety information."

The slightly older man laughed gently. "I have known you for, let me see, is it fifty years, or fifty-five, Jim? I would warrant that ten minutes ago you were with your closest advisers and that you didn't like what developed."

Number One exhaled smoke through his nostrils. Abruptly he said, "Graves gave his final report. The computers say the war would be over in less than three months. We would take about 330,000 casualties, of which some 18,000 would be deaths."

"I see. And how many would the defenders of Betastan lose?"

"I didn't ask."

"You should have," the Temple Monk said softly.

"Not before such Coaids as Marshal Croft-Gordon and our Surety bloodhound, Mark Fielder. It would be interpreted as an unbelievable weakness in a Presidor."

Pater Riggin looked at him thoughtfully. "I can anticipate what most of them reported and recommended, Jim. Were any at all in opposition?"

"Ross, perhaps."

"Franklin's boy, eh? And what was our Deputy of Propaganda's position?"

"He thought we were going to have our work cut out selling an aggressive war not only to the neutrals but to our own people. He thinks it all comes too soon after the civil war Max precipitated."

The Temple Monk shook his head, weariness there. "Would that he were right."

Number One looked at him, saying nothing.

The Temple Monk opened the book at the page he had been perusing. "Jim, have you ever heard of a writer named Mark Twain?"

"I don't believe so."

17

"Early Earth. Many an unthinking person, seeing only his surface, thought him a humorist. Basically, he wasn't. He was an idealist and crusader who died a very bitter man. Listen to this." He read.

" 'The loud little handful—as usual—will shout for the war. The pulpit will—warily and cautiously—object —at first; the great, big, dull bulk of the nation will rub its sleepy eyes and try to make out why there should be a war, and will say, earnestly and indignantly, *It is unjust and dishonorable, and there is no necessity for it.* Then the handful will shout louder. A few fair men on the other side will argue and reason against the war with speech and pen, and at first will have a hearing and be applauded; but it will not last long; those others will outshout them, and presently the antiwar audience will thin out and lose popularity. Before long you will see this curious thing: the speakers stoned from the platform, and free speech strangled by hordes of furious men who in their secret hearts are still at one with those stoned speakers—as earlier—but do not dare to say so. And now the whole nation—pulpit and all—will take up the war cry, and shout itself hoarse, and mob any honest man who ventures to open his mouth; and presently such mouths will cease to open. Next, the statesmen will invent cheap lies, putting the blame upon the nation that is attacked, and every man will be glad of these conscience-soothing falsities, and will diligently study them, and refuse to examine any refutations of them; and thus he will by and by convince himself that the war is just, and will thank God for the better sleep he enjoys after this process of grotesque self-deception.' "

Pater Riggin looked up, closing the book again.

"It was true in Twain's time, and much more so today. Given the well disciplined press, given well channeled Tri-Di shows and news broadcasts, given a people that have been raised since earliest childhood in the chauvinistic belief that their country is always right;

and even if it isn't they should support it—given these, and you can have your war, Jim. Of course, if it lasted too long, then there would be reaction. But so long as the man in the street isn't too badly put out, you can have your war, Number One."

The other pretended to miss the term. He said, "Rig, you know Phil McGivern."

The Temple Monk said wryly, "Our authority on socioeconomics."

"His computers tell him that without new foreign markets and sources of raw material we face an economic collapse in a few months. The system won't take it, Rig."

His lifelong companion looked at him unblinkingly.

Number One continued, an undertone of urgency in his voice as though pleading for understanding. "It would mean more civil disorders, Rig. More fighting in the streets. More of the bloodbath we had when Max and his group tried to take over."

The Temple Monk looked away. He and his present companion had never discussed, more than in passing, the *coup d'état* attempted by their mutual friend, Maximilian Barker.

He said gently, "Possibly Max had the right idea and we didn't realize it at the time."

"What is that supposed to mean?" the Presidor rasped. "You can push our friendship too far, Pater Riggin. Max was a damned rabid Karlist, and you know it!"

Pater Riggin shook his head, unimpressed by the sudden heat. "No, I don't. All I know is that your Commissariats of Surety and Information branded him such, and over and over again, and loudly, and to the skies. Until, possibly, even you believed them. It's a dangerous thing, Jim, to believe your own propaganda, but it comes to all men if they listen to it long enough."

Number One came suddenly to his feet. He threw the half smoked stogie down, missing the ash tray. The

19

long slim cigar hit the table and rolled across it to drop unheeded on the floor beyond.

The ultimate head of Alphaland strode angrily to the bar, took up the bottle from which he had poured earlier, on his first entry into the room, and poured again, this time into a tumbler. He threw the potent brandy back over his palate, grimaced and turned to a bank of dials, levers and buttons set next to a bookcase.

He snarled at his friend, "The ultimate computer. The foolproof adviser. The computer designed for the layman."

He snatched up a hand mike and roared into it. "In the event that war is not provoked with Betastan within two months, what will the result be so far as the Presidor is concerned?"

The answer came from the speaker so quickly that it would seem that the angry man's voice had scarcely died away.

"The likelihood of armed revolt against the present occupant of the office is ninety-one point eight percent, give or take one point four percent."

"Who would lead such a revolt?"

"The likelihood is that the revolt would be led by one or a combination of two or more of three men: Deputies Matheison and Fielder and Marshal Croft-Gordon."

"Would such a revolt be successful?"

"The likelihood of the revolt's success would be eighty-two percent, give or take three point three percent."

"In the case of the revolt's success, what would be the likelihood of a war then being undertaken against Betastan?"

"Ninety-six percent, give or take two point one percent."

He slammed down the hand mike into its cradle and began to turn to his companion, but then he said, "No!" and took it up again.

"Would the United Temple support the government of the current Presidor if he declared war upon Betastan?"

"The likelihood is ninety-eight point six percent that the United Temple would support the Presidor, give or take one-half of one percent."

Number One turned back to his only intimate and now his Prussian starched shoulders had slipped into resignation.

"So you see, even the Holy Ultimate, through his representatives on this planet, supports the war. Any ideas, Rig?"

Tilly Trice looked over the newcomer and made a wryly humorous moue.

"You don't look like much of a soldier, Centurion," she said.

He said ungraciously, "Neither do you. Isn't that part of the idea?"

"How old are you, anyway?"

His youthful face was petulant. "That's none of your business."

Her fine eyebrows went up. "Tu, tu, tu. You're talking to a superior officer, Centurion."

"Yes, sir. I mean . . ."

The slightly built girl laughed. "I never felt right about that either. However, the correct term is madam."

"Yes, sir." The other flushed. "I mean madam. Trouble is, you don't look like a madam." He jerked his head in alarm. "That is . . ."

She laughed again. "All right, let's cut out this jetsam. Wait'll I change my clothes, and we'll get going." She ran her eyes over him critically. "You look all right." She thought of something. "Are you carrying a shooter?"

"Of course."

"Well, ditch it, right here and now. Are you drivel

21

happy? You think you're going to get into a government building carrying as much metal as that?"

She indicated a desk. "Stick it in there." She turned to go into the next room, the living quarters behind her store.

He put the gun into a drawer, scowling. "There's no way of locking this. Anybody snooping around would see it."

Just before she passed through the door she looked back at him scornfully and said, "Centurion Combs, face reality. If Alphaland Surety ever became suspicious enough to start seriously snooping around this place they'd find so much that the jig'd be up. One shooter, more or less, wouldn't make an iota."

She left and he spent the next ten minutes staring at the shelves of books. He had never seen this many outside of a museum. He took one or two down from the shelves and handled them gingerly. He decided it must have been a tedious way of reading.

When Tilly returned he looked at her for a moment, frowning, obviously in lack of recognition.

"Knock it." She laughed, in a just-short-of giggle. "It's me."

He stared at her, his eyes going up and down her masculine costume. Finally, for lack of something else, he demanded, "Where'd you get those buck teeth?"

She snorted, "Centurion, I don't know where you received your ECE training. Cosmetics can whip up a guise like this before you could get down a glass of guzzle."

"I don't drink," he said righteously. "Besides, I didn't study at the Espionage-Counter-Espionage Academy."

"Come on, let's get going," she said, handing him a piece of fruit. "Where did you study?" She headed for the door.

He followed her, looking at the thing in his hand. "What's this? I studied at Partisan Tech."

22

There was a sporty looking hover-scooter at the curb.

She said, "You get on back. Keep your eyes open. You're going to want to learn this town, inside out. If you ever have any spare time, walk or ride up and down the streets, memorizing them. It might mean your life someday."

"Well, all right. Look, what do we want with a banana?"

"Hang on," she said, dropping the lift lever. "It's part of our protective covering. The one little added bit of business that puts us over."

He was sitting behind her. He rolled his eyes upward, as though surrendering to idiocy on the part of superior authority.

They slammed down the boulevard at a speed that must have been in excess of city ordinances.

"Hey, uh, madam," he protested finally. "You want to get picked up by some Alpha fuzz-yoke?"

"No," she told him. "But this is part of the protective coloring, too. Looks authentic."

She zoomed finally into the parking zone of a monstrous stone building and skittered to a halt.

Tilly vaulted from her seat exuberantly.

"Come on!" she said.

He followed her, more sedate. "This says it's for Senior Personnel only," he whispered.

"I know, I know. Let's go."

"Hey, you two kids!" a voice called impatiently. "You can't leave that scooter there."

"Aw, why not?" Tilly whined.

A uniformed Surety officer came up. He snapped, "Because I said so, damn it."

Tilly put her hands on her hips belligerently. "Listen, do you know who my father is?"

A weary expression came over his face. He was a heavy, bullyboy type, a quick-draw holster built into his leather jacket where a left pocket might have been.

23

But obviously this was no occasion for weight being thrown around.

He said, "No, sonny, my heart is pumping curd, but I don't know who your daddy is. All I know, if Superintendent Nichols comes in here and finds that souped-up scooter in his parking place, he'll burn off."

"I'm just gonna be here for a minute," Tilly whined.

Her companion got into the act. "Aw, come on, Killer," he said. "Don't argue with this cloddy. Park it somewhere else."

The Surety man eyed him unhappily, opened his mouth as though to growl something, but then shrugged it off.

"Snap it up, boys," he said. "You just can't leave it here."

"All right, all right," Tilly said. "Give me a hand, Bimbo." She and Combs took hold of the sports hover and pushed it down the line to a public parking zone.

They then headed for the entrance, where two additional Surety men, both with scrambler rifles, stood post. They had lazily been watching the hassle with the parking attendant.

Tilly said, "Peel your banana." She pulled her own piece of fruit from her pocket and began to eat it.

Combs asked, "Why all that, back there?"

"Protective coloring," she said.

They climbed the half dozen stone steps and began entering the building.

"Halt!" one of the guards barked.

"Aw, curd," Tilly sneered, continuing on her way.

"I said halt, damn it! Where do you kids think you're going?"

Tilly's face fell into the expression, known since man issued forth from the caves of Cro-Magnon, of the teen-ager being put upon.

"Aw," she whined. "I gotta see my old man. Holy

Jumping Zen, I don't have all morning. I gotta lot of things to do. I'm supposed to see my old man."

The other guard said, "You can't go in here, buster. This is government . . ."

The first guard interrupted him. "Who's your father, and what are you supposed to see him about?"

"He forgot his pills."

The long-suffering Surety man rubbed his mouth.

Eating his banana, a sneer of superiority on his face, Combs said, "Aw, the hell with it. Killer. Let's go see if we can scare up a couple mopsies."

Tilly said, argumentive, "My old lady said I gotta get these pills to my old man. He'll drop dead, yet, or something. He's been taking these pills till they run outa his ears. I never seen them do him any good."

The second guard said, "What's your father's name, sonny?"

Combs chucked. "Sonny, yet, he calls you, Killer."

Tilly said, "My old man's Assistant Supervisor Hillary. He swings a lot of weight around this crumby joint, fella."

"I never heard of him," the first guard said hesitantly.

"I have. I'll phone up," the other one said.

"Aw, curd," Tilly said. "You'll take halfa the morning. I know where he is. I know everybody in the department. He wanders around a lot between the offices. I can find him."

"Let him go, let him go," the one guard said to the other. "Zen, what difference does it make?"

Tilly waited no longer. She and her companion headed for the door again, still eating their bananas. The second guard muttered something, but they were through the entrance.

Combs said, "Whee. Suppose they'd phoned up to this Supervisor Hillary? Is there any such cloddy?"

She shot him an impish grin. "Sure. You think I'm inefficient? I happen to know that Hillary left the building by another entrance and at this moment is being entertained by his mistress, half a dozen kilometers from here. If they phoned up to his office, his secretary, who covers for him, would have said he was wandering around the building, checking on his underlings."

Combs shook his head.

They moped along down the building's corridors, drawing only the slightest attention from bustling bureaucrats, secretaries, building maintenance workers, and the others who teemed the halls.

They got to the part of the building which was their destination and had to saunter up and down a couple of times until the way was clear.

Tilly opened a door and they hurried inside. She barred it behind them.

"We've got to work moderately fast," she said. "Prove your worth, Centurion."

"Where in Zen's the line?"

"Here, help me push this box away. There you are. I assume you can get that open?"

"I can get anything open." The youthful looking Betastan operative bent down to look at the metal aperture set into the wall. "How'd you ever locate this?"

"My dear boy," Tilly said, "in a country like this, where the gold Alpha is almighty, spreading them around a bit will buy you just about anything at all."

He was on his knees working at the tiny door. It swung open to reveal wires beyond.

Tilly said, mildly impressed, "How'd you open that?"

"Hairpin," he said absently.

Combs opened his jerkin and brought forth a device from an inner garment that resembled a many compartmented money belt. He was humming sourly to himself as he worked.

"Don't think it all goes this easily," Tilly said. "There isn't much of a Surety guard about the Commissariat of Information."

"Hmmmm," he murmured, not really hearing her.

It was a full two hours later when they emerged from the building maintenance room. Tilly came out first, shot her eyes up and down the corridor.

"Hurry," she said.

Combs began to emerge, still stuffing some of his equipment back into his compartmented belt.

At that split moment, a uniformed Surety guard, trailing a scrambler gun at ease, rounded the nearest corner of the hall. It was one of the two who had been posted at the entry.

He came to a halt and blinked at them.

"Hey," he snapped. "What're you two kids doing, eh? What in Zen're you still doing in the building?"

Tilly walked toward him. "Aw," she said. "I couldn't find my old man at first. He was out gettin' a bite, or somethin'."

Combs slouched along behind her. "Yeah," he sneered. "We're spendin' the whole day around this crumby . . ."

The guard snapped, "What were you doing in that . . ."

Tilly dove for his legs, throwing what little heft she had into the attempt to bring him to the floor.

Behind her, Combs leaped, his hands held chopper fashion.

The guard tumbled, too astonished to yell.

One chopper slashed out, and the guard's larynx collapsed. Combs banged him again, behind the ear this time.

Breathing deep, the two Betastan agents came to their feet.

Tilly was pale. "We've got to work fast," she said. "If we're caught, they've got the perfect excuse to start the war. Public opinion throughout the neutrals . . ." She let the sentence fade. "Come on."

27

She had grabbed one foot of the dead man. He took the other.

"Where're we going?" he demanded, breathing heavily. "Somebody'll come along this hall . . ."

"Here," she said. They'd reached a stairway.

They pushed the Surety man down, letting him roll over and over again.

"Quick," she said. "The gun."

Combs scurried back and got the scrambler. They tossed it after their victim.

"Just a minute. I thought of something," Tilly whispered. She scurried back to the room they had just left, while Combs' eyes darted up and down the deserted hallway. It was lunch time, but you never knew.

She came back, one of the banana skins in her hands.

She put it on the top step, put her foot over it and rubbed it flat, as though it had been stepped upon accidently.

"Come on, Centurion, let's get out of here," she said.

He looked at her, even as they scurried from the scene. "That was no joke when I called you Killer," he said.

III

THE GUARD at the door clicked his heels and said, "Co-aid Deputy Ross Westley."

Number One looked up from the work on his desk.

Ross entered and came to attention, even though he was dressed in mufti.

"Your Leadership," he said.

The guard closed the door behind him.

Number One nodded. "Sit down, Ross."

"Yes, Your Leadership." Ross Westley crossed nearer to the quarter acre of desk behind which his ultimate superior sat, and found himself a chair. He had heard once that Number One deliberately had the chairs in his sanctum sanctorum constructed to be uncomfortable —possibly working on the theory that he didn't want people about him to be at ease, physically or mentally. Ross didn't know, but uncomfortable the chairs were.

Number One looked at him bleakly. "The decision has been made. Your commissariat has exactly one month in which to prepare the people for our crusade against Betastan."

"A month!" Ross blurted.

"We can afford no more. I wish your father were still alive, Ross, but since he isn't I trust your own ability to handle this."

"Your Leadership," Ross said tightly. "I doubt if my father, even, could have drummed up a war fever in this country in as short a period as one month. What possible approach . . ."

The Presidor eyed him grimly. "That is the problem of your offices, Coaid. You will receive full cooperation from all departments."

Ross Westley's mouth worked, but he could think of nothing to say.

"Snap out of it," the other rumbled in sudden irritation. "There are thousands of approaches. Consult your staff. Bauserman would have a dozen suggestions by this time."

A dozen? Ross thought bitterly. A double-score was more like it. Each more repulsive than the last.

Number One now said, "One suggestion of my own. The United Temple is fully behind this crusade. In fact"—he smiled his humorless smile—"His Holiness himself suggested that we call it just that, a Crusade. You realize that in the past century, in particular, the Betastani have drifted away from the more orthodox dogmas of the United Temple. I would play upon the fact, concentrate upon it, that our most basic desire in the war to defend ourselves against the Betastan ag-

29

gressors is to bring back the true faith to that benighted land."

Ross winced. "Isn't that going to be a bit hard to swallow? Not on the part of the Betastani, of course. They don't count. But the neutrals?"

"That is your task, Ross. Your commissariat had carte blanche. The computers have put your budget at approximately sixty-three million Alphas."

The Presidor took a deep breath. "I suppose that is all for the moment. We shall have a session of the inmost coaids this afternoon and shall devote part of it to your propaganda campaign. By then, I assume you will have at least a skeletal program to present to us."

Ross Westley came to his feet. "Yes, Your Leadership. With your permission."

"Until this afternoon," Number One said.

Ross Westley slumped at the head of the table while his assistant, Job Bauserman, briefed department heads of the Commissariat of Information on the orders which had come directly from Number One.

He followed Assistant Deputy Bauserman sourly. The other was a full ten years the senior of Ross Westley and had come up in the governmental branch from the near bottom. He was lean and fanatic, had a gleaming eye and an overpowering ambition—and hated his superior's guts.

It had been, of course, a matter of nepotism. Franklin Westley, the father of Ross, had been one of the Old Hands—those who had stood shoulder to shoulder with Number One on the barricades of the first rebellion. He was one of those who had remained true when the Max Barker revolt burst into flames and even the Old Hands had been split.

The Old Hands took care of their own. When Franklin Westley died, Ross had been given his position as Deputy of the Commissariat of Information, known in party circles as the Department of Propaganda. At the time he received the appointment, shortly after taking his doctor's degree in ancient history, his knowledge of the office was exactly nil. In time he had learned, but it was Job Bauserman and the others who were long-time pros upon whom he had to lean. He knew it and they knew it. And most of them hated him. Surely, Job did.

The other turned to Ross finally and, forced respect in his voice, said, "Have you anything to add to my summary, Coaid Deputy?"

Ross shook his head and sat more erect. His assistant took his chair.

Ross said, "One month. I needn't tell you that we're going to need every second of it. This afternoon, there's a meeting of the Central Comita. I've got to have at least a skeleton program to present. All right, ideas, please."

Pater Ian said, "The United Temple has in its infinite wisdom long foreseen this development. The erring brethren of Betastan must be brought back into the fold. Of recent months we have been studying the workings of a historic organization which, under somewhat similar circumstances, proved highly effective. It was called the Holy Office. However, this plan of operation will not be practical until the collapse of the Betastani resistance. Meanwhile, the United Temple plans to open a full drive, not only in Alphaland and Betaland, but among the neutrals as well, revealing the extent to which the Betastani government has allowed atheism and agnosticism to undermine the faith of the people. If you will find time, Coaid Deputy, I shall go over in detail our broadcasts, publications and so forth, detailing the campaign.

Ross nodded. "Tomorrow morning, please." He turned to another department head. "Coaid Taylor?"

Martha Taylor was the dry, neuter-sex type prevalent in governmental higher ranks.

31

She said, "I think I have something good. The Amish."

Ross scowled at her. "The Amish?"

"To brief you, Coaid Deputy, I found this in my department's data banks, somewhat to my surprise. It would seem that when the planet was first being colonized from Mother Earth, one ship's complement was composed of a somewhat discriminated against religious group which settled in the back areas of Betastan near the Tatra Mountains. Later, elements of this group diffused over the planet, though few came to Alphaland."

"Never heard of them," somebody growled. "What's this got to do with drumming up war fever against the damned Betastan funkers?"

She rewarded the speaker with a scornful eye, but went on. "The reason they had been discriminated against soon became obvious. They stuck together against all outside pressures. They went into such fields as finance and merchandising, soon gaining all but monopolies not only in Betastan but in several other nations. They also gained high governmental offices, though usually inconspicuous ones. Evidently, from my data, they are the power behind the Betastan administration."

Ross was frowning. "The Amish?"

"That is the common name given their pseudo-religious group, Coaid Deputy," she said stiffly.

Ross said, shaking his head, "When I was a boy, I went once to the Tatra Mountains on a vacation. Skiing. I didn't get to know any personally, but I failed to gain your picture of these people. They were rather drably dressed and not overly gregarious perhaps . . ."

"That's what I am saying, Coaid. Evidently they're almost like misers, hoarding their finances, associating only with each other. And, to top it all, they have their own false religion, not abiding by the benevolent guidance of the United Temple."

"Hmmmm," Pater Ian injected. "It seems to me that I have vaguely heard of this group. However, I didn't think their powers extended as far as you report."

"The data banks hardly lie, Pater," she said primly.

"No, of course not," The Temple Monk said.

Assistant Deputy Bauserman came into it, his eyes gleaming. "It's a natural. There's absolutely nothing like religion to get people steamed up to the boiling point. Remember the Hindus and Moslems, back on Earth? Supposedly, a Hindu wouldn't swat a mosquito since it would be breaking the taboo against taking life, but given religious troubles with the Moslems and they slaughtered and were slaughtered by the millions. Or take the centuries-long wars and massacres between the Christian sects; all in the name of the gentle Jesus, they butchered each other wholesale. Or take the Christian prosecution of the Jews, down through the millennia. No, religion is the perfect background for butchery."

"My son," Pater Ian said in mild protest.

Bauserman looked at him. "Oh, I didn't mean the Holy United Temple, Pater Ian. Obviously, at long last man has evolved to the perfect intermediary between himself and God. However, from what Coaid Taylor says, this Amish scum doesn't even observe the leadership of the United Temple in matters religious. They are fair game in this holy crusade we are about to embark upon."

The Temple Monk nodded thoughtfully. "It would seem so."

Ross exhaled air. He had no alternative. He said, "All right, Coaid Taylor. I will expect your department to launch a full denouncement of these Amish. For three weeks you will exploit every opportunity to expose them. At the end of the period, stress the sacred need for all believers in the true religion to seek these Amish out and destroy them."

33

Bauserman broke in. "You might also continually hint that they are actually part of the Karlist conspiracy."

Ross looked at him. "What Karlist conspiracy, Job?" He seldom used the other's first name, knowing Bauserman's objection to anything less than the strictest form, but it had come out in his surprise.

His Assistant Deputy turned to him. "I was about to brief you on this phase, Coaid Deputy Westley. Obviously, we are going to have to devote a major part of our propaganda campaign to the Karlist threat. It will be particularly effective among the neutrals. Just the mention of the word is enough to set governments trembling in half the nations on the planet. We'll push the line that the Betastan government is infiltrated with Amish and Karlists. That there's a scheme underfoot to allow the Karlists to take over the government and then subvert the rest of the world."

Somebody muttered, "I thought there weren't enough Karlists left in the world to hold a committee meeting."

Bauserman looked at the speaker coldly. "Coaid, the ends justify the means. The holy crusade to bring the whole planet under the aegis of our inspired Presidor is an effort so worthy that nothing done to achieve its success can be thought of as less than the truth in the ultimate sense of the word."

"I could not have stated it better myself," Pater Ian said unctuously.

"All right," Ross sighed. "You can go over this with me later in detail, Coaid Bauserman. And now, what else do we have as possible propaganda against the Betastani?"

A uniformed colonel said, "Off and on, over the years, we've had touches of border trouble. It could be allowed to come to a boil."

"How?"

The colonel looked at his superior as though the other

were stupid, then caught himself and his face went militarily blank.

"Several ways, Coaid Deputy. We could precipitate a clash with their border guards, and then claim they had started it. We could escalate the clash, over and over again—always assuming the funkers would resist at all.

"Or, we could infiltrate a few score of our ECE men, armed with mortars, at one of the least populated border points, and let them shell one of our own garrisons or towns. The mortar shells, of course, would be Betastan calibers and we would make sure some of them failed to explode. We could then bring a planet-wide committee to see the effects of the shelling, the dead and wounded civilians, old men, women, children—that sort of thing. A hospital would be good. A shelled hospital is particularly effective in the way of horrifying non-combatants. I've never quite figured out why."

The Temple Monk said gently, "My sons, couldn't some more kindly tactics be devised? Not that I wish to inject a note that interferes with secular affairs. The United Temple is involved only with man's most spiritual concerns."

They ignored him.

Bauserman, his eyes gleaming, said, "A natural, Colonel!"

Ross Westley left his pneumatic car at the park entry and, ignoring his usual precautions, made his way in the direction of the bookshop and binding service presided over by Tilly Trice. He didn't notice the two unobtrusive men in civilian clothing who drifted after him.

After he had disappeared into her tiny store, one of the two tails looked at the other, eyebrows raised.

The second one said, "Better report."

"What've we got to report? The chief said to follow him. All he's done is go into an antique bookstore."

"Listen, if you were in the frame of mind he oughta be in these days, would you be going into a bookstore? Some bootleg auto-bar, yeah. Even a mopsy-house, yeah. But an antique bookstore?"

The other grunted.

The first said contemptuously, "The flat. No precautions at all. Doesn't even look over his shoulder."

The other said sourly, "Which indicates he wasn't thinking in terms of having anything to hide."

"Well, let's go report. There's something funny about that old bookshop. Come to think of it, that's one of the places Admiral Korshak used to go before he committed suicide."

"He did! Holy Ultimate, let's get to a communicator."

The other looked around nervously. "Watch your lip, Larry. Just because you're Surety doesn't mean some Temple Monk cloddy might not nail you for blasphemy."

They started back the way they had come.

The one who had been contemptuous of Ross Westley's lack of caution could have taken a lesson from his own teachings. Neither of the two Surety agents had noticed the three teen-agers who had been strolling across the street from them but in the same direction, even though the three loudly dressed youngsters had been noisy enough, conspicuous enough.

Nor did they see the three close in behind them.

Nor did they see the one who raised to his lips what seemed to be a bean-shooter.

Tilly Trice pouted at him. "Nope, lover-mine, I told you. I can't marry you until this crisis is past. Even then, I'm still thinking about it. Your passion, fella, is obvious. But any girl should know that first passion can pass. How'll you be in the long pull, Rossie, my friend?"

"Look," he blurted, "you know damn well you're the only girl that ever made any difference to me."

"Tu, tu, tu. And now who's using four letter words?"

He looked at her blankly.

"Damn," she said.

He tried to follow along with her lighter mood, knowing full well that in her presence he was apt to become miserably dull, absorbed in his need for her.

"I thought it was a three letter word," he said. He crossed her heart and pointed upward. "May the Holy Ultimate strike me dead if I ever use a four letter word to you again."

Her eyebrows rose, even as she put the book she had been recovering to the side. "Your stock just went up," she said. "I thought you were a fully indoctrinated follower of the United Temple."

He growled, "That's for the yokes."

"Oh? Is that the common belief among you deputies? I understood that Number One in particular was never without a Temple Monk by his side."

Ross scoffed contempt. "It's my department that spreads that bit of gobbledygook. Actually, Pater Riggin is an old-time friend of the Presidor's. They bat the breeze around about top decisions but so far as religion is concerned, I doubt if either of them has attended conclave for the past ten years."

She said suddenly, "What develops, Rossie?"

He looked at her, his face sullen now. "It's set. One month to go. Listen, Till, get out from under. Marry me. Call it all quits. I can cover for you indefinitely. Betastan is sunk. According to Marshal Croft-Gordon we have the military and industrial potential to take Betastan three times over. Three times, Till! What you've got to do is use what influence you've got to get your country to capitulate. Otherwise, when the initial missile and air attack takes place, Betastan has had it to the tune of millions of casualties."

Her eyes were first narrow, but her expression faded into the thoughtful.

"If I'm reading you correctly, Rossie, there's to be a sneak attack."

"I shouldn't have revealed that," he said, still sullen. "But you might have guessed."

"Where do you draw the line?" She laughed mockingly at him. "You've been giving me information for months."

"Trying to enable you to get out from under. But now it's getting to the point where there's no alternative. Each man's got to take his stand, Till. And Betastan hasn't got a chance. I was a fool to help you at all."

She said, after pursing her lips, "I'll tell you, Rossie. Maybe you've got a point. But it'd be a mistake, the sneak attack. Bad propaganda. You should know that, it's your field. You ought to give some slight warning. Any warning at all would look better to the neutrals. At least it gives us the chance to back down before your, uh, might."

"You're right!" Ross said. "I'll have to bring that up. Then you think there's a chance your government will capitulate? But look, why don't you drop it all and marry me?"

She looked down at her meager figure as though in surprise. "What is there about little Tilly Trice that moves the overgrown cloddy just so?"

"It's no joke, Till!"

She let her bright face go serious. "I know, Rossie, but that's the way the water flows. As I told you, when all this trouble is over, well, then possibly there'll be me."

IV

It was the last session of the Central Comita of the Free Democratic Commonwealth of Alphaland previous to C-Day, the day during which the Crusade, the

38

liberation of Betastan from its depraved Karlist-Amish government, would commence.

Marshal of the Armies Rupert Croft-Gordon, using his swagger stick to point out on small scale military charts the points of attack, had been holding forth. His talk was punctuated with the figures his computers had come up with, plus or minus this amount, plus or minus that percentage. The Marshal, it was obvious, was in fine fettle. A man does not study a science, if the military be science, for a lifetime without yearning to put his pet theories into practice.

He came to an end, at long last, hit his swagger stick against his leggings with a quick double rap, and said, "Questions, Coaids?"

Number One said, very evenly, "You will address *me,* Coaid Marshal. *I* shall decide whether or not at this point we shall have a session of questions."

Croft-Gordon flushed darkly. "Yes, Your Leadership. That is what I meant. Does Your Leadership have any questions to ask?"

Number One looked at him thoughtfully and for a long moment. Once the dogs of war are let loose, he well knew, none can say what will transpire before they are in leash again. And the military mind is ever ambitious. Number One was not so naïve as not to know that Marshal Croft-Gordon dreamed of ultimate power, and that various of the deputies supported him in their secret hearts. Number One had no need of a computer to tell him that.

He took in the unhappy face of Ross Westley.

"Coaid, you wish to speak? I hope your contribution is somewhat more efficacious than the farce your commissariat precipitated in regard to the so-called Amish threat."

Ross shook his head. "Your Leadership, perhaps we can all take a lesson from that—not to underestimate the enemy."

"Jetsam," Mark Fielder of Surety snorted.

Ross looked at him. "It was no easy romp on the part of the Betastani to infiltrate the Commissariat of Information and feed false data into our banks. We proceeded on the basis of that data. How were we to know that in actuality the Amish are small in number in Betastan, invariably well-thought-of by their neighbors, not interested in accumulating large amounts of property and having no interest whatsoever in government? The worst result of our misinformation, of course, was neither in Alphaland or Betastan, but in the two or three neutral nations where there are large Amish elements."

He directed his gaze, somewhat apologetically, at the Presidor, and held up a report tape.

"Your Leadership, immediately before entering this meeting I received final news on the overthrow of the pro-Alphaland government of Moravia. The revolt is completely successful and the new regime leans toward Betastan. We have, of course, branded it Karlist."

Number One said, "Ordinarily, we would have sent in airborne marines to preserve liberty, but at this point we can afford to divert no considerable number of effectives. We shall have to deal with Moravia following the Crusade."

Deputy Matheison jiggled his stylo. "Are they really Karlists?"

Ross shook his head. "No, Coaid. But the new government is so liberal that it just misses being so labeled. The more notorious anti-Alphaland elements all support it."

Number One said, "I assume the point you wished to raise didn't deal with this now past matter of the anti-Amish propaganda."

Ross turned back to his ultimate superior. "No, Your Leadership. I rose to protest the sneak attack the Marshal proposes. The plan to strike all their most important cities, industrial complexes and military bases without warning."

"What!" Croft-Gordon barked. "Our whole campaign . . . !"

Number One held up a hand. "That will be all, Coaid Marshal."

He turned back to Ross. "Develop your point, Coaid Westley."

Ross went on doggedly. "We have already had a bad start on our propaganda meant to influence our own people, the neutrals and dissatisfied elements among the Betastani. An attack without a previous formal declaration of war will unite the Betastani, shock our own people who are poorly prepared for this aggressive war at any rate, and will certainly turn the neutrals against us."

The Central Comita broke into mutterings.

Number One said, "Marshal?"

The Marshal said heatedly, "The plans have all been explained. The computers have worked on the basis of such a surprise. . . . I resent the Coaid Deputy's use of the term 'sneak attack.' Without it we would still triumph easily, of course, but the cost in casualties and finances would inevitably be higher."

Ross said, "It will be higher still if the neutrals enter the war on the side of Betastan."

"You heard the report Graves gave on that. They won't have the time to mobilize, even if they did want to enter. The war will be over in weeks."

Number One was irritated by the overriding inflection of his military chief. He said, thoughtfully, "We could send them an ultimatum concerning their unprovoked attacks upon our border stations. It could be worded in such a way that they wouldn't actually expect us to attack. However, we could hold a secret session of the Peoples Parliament and declare war and have our missiles and bombers on the way within minutes. Public opinion would be satisfied, but at the same time the attack would have practically the same effect as if no warning had been given."

He looked about at his Comita members. "If there are no other opinions, I so rule."

The Marshal opened his mouth angrily, shut it again and shook his head.

Number One said, "Are there further questions at this point?"

Deputy Mark Fielder of the Commissariat of Surety came easily to his feet.

"This bears on the present issue only obliquely, Your Leadership. However, since Coaid Westley was the last speaker . . ." He took up a report from before him.

"There has been so obvious an increase in enemy ECE, Espionage-Counter-Espionage, so many leaks of our innermost secrets to Betastan, that I have taken the freedom to check upon all elements who might possibly be involved. Even, Your Leadership, to the point of, ah, keeping tabs upon our membership."

There was the sound of inhaled air throughout the council room.

Number One's eyes were cold. "We have been through this before, Coaid Fielder. You seem to have ignored my earlier directives."

Fielder said smoothly, "If so, inadvertently, Your Leadership. Please hear me out. Purely as routine check I assigned two of my most discreet men to observe the activities of each of us."

"Including yourself, I assume," the Presidor said. "Go on, Coaid. I suppose you found Coaid Wilkonson, or possibly Academecian McGivern, secretly supplying information to the Betastan espionage."

Fielder was not upset. He shook his head. "No, Your Leadership, but something equally strange. The two Surety agents who were assigned to Coaid Westley disappeared while on duty and were eventually found

42

trampled beyond easy recognition in the pachyderm exhibit at the Interplanetary Zoo."

"What's a pachyderm?" someone said.

The Surety head looked at the speaker. "A large Earthside animal, now extinct except for specimens in zoos." He brought his eyes back to Number One. "But that is not all. In spite of the condition of the bodies, an autopsy was performed. Both contained elements of the drug popularly known as Come-Along, an ultra-effective hypnotic."

Number One took in Ross Westley from the side of his eyes. The young propaganda chief was sitting in mute astonishment, his mouth half open. In the decision of his ultimate superior, who considered himself a judge of men, the younger deputy was as taken aback as anyone present.

Number One said, his voice harsh, "Your recommendation, Coaid Deputy Fielder?"

"That Coaid Westley be put under Scop and questioned."

Number One lapsed into thought and the murmuring immediately hushed. For long minutes they stayed that way, Deputy Fielder still on his feet, but hesitant even to sink into his chair.

Ross Westley felt the cold go through him. Given Scop, he would betray not only himself, but Tilly as well. There was no question of that. No man resisted the insidiousness of the truth serum. He must think of some out! He must think of some escape.

But there was no thinking, there was no out!

Number One, though his face was expressionless, was in a fury. Mark Fielder and Marshal Croft-Gordon were becoming increasingly bold in their formerly subtle opposition to his supreme command. Nothing overt thus far, but when the pressures of the war were on Alphaland, to what extent would they continue to undermine his authority? They must be sat upon, and quickly. He considered, momentarily, relieving them both of their positions. But no, a purge at this time would be disastrous. The effects upon the people, immediately before an unpopular war, could only be a blow to morale. It had been such a long time since the Central Comita had suffered a purge that many thought them a thing of the past.

At long last, the Presidor spoke again, his voice deceptively mild.

"Coaid Fielder, only a short time ago it was brought to our attention that you had seen fit to bug the offices and living quarters of even these, your most intimate Coaids. At that time I pointed out that if my regime rested upon the shoulders of Coaids who had to be kept under surveillance by the Commissariat of Surety, then the government of the Free Democratic Commonwealth was built upon foundations of sand. Coaid Westley, young and possibly somewhat inexperienced as he may be, is the son of Franklin Westley, one of the Old Hands. Perhaps the term is meaningless to you, but it is not to such Coaids present as McGivern and Wilkonson, both of whom stood shoulder to shoulder with Franklin Westley in the decisive days. The son of Franklin Westley will not be given Scop in my behalf, nor will any of the Central Comita."

There was a murmuring of applause through the chamber.

Temple Bishop Stockwater said soothingly, "Undoubtedly, whilst about their duties, the two Surety operatives of whom Coaid Fielder tells us ran into criminals or enemy agents, and in dealing with them met their untimely ends."

"Undoubtedly," Fielder muttered. He bowed his head in submission to the Presidor's decision.

Ross Westley burst into the tiny shop devoted to first

editions, old prints, bookbinding and the literature of the past.

He called, "Tilly, Till!" heading for the back rooms.

He had crossed the shop and pushed through into her private quarters before she fully realized his presence.

Tilly Trice was in the process of pulling a masculine shirt over the top of her head and the upper part of her diminutive, elfin figure.

He came to a quick halt and blinked at the woman he loved.

She turned her back and finished tucking the garment into her trousers.

"Why, Coaid Westley," she said, mockery behind the scolding, "aren't you a bit impetuous?" She took up a jerkin and began shrugging into it.

Ross began to stutter an apology but then cut himself short. Against the table leaned a long bow, and on it rested a quiver of arrows.

He said, "What in the world are you doing in that get-up, and what's wrong with your teeth?"

She pursed her lips, and there was a mischievous quality in the look she shot him from the side of her eyes.

"Life-long ambition," she said. "Archery."

"But . . . but what are you doing in that outfit? And what's wrong with your teeth? You look like a buck-toothed juvenile delinquent."

She said, "Suppose I make it all very simple, Rossie. Let's say the only archery club worthwhile in this town is for boys only. No curves allowed. So, what could be simpler? I pretend I'm a teen-age boy. The teeth? Oh, it's an added disguise. Otherwise, somebody might recognize me."

In a way, he was hearing the truth—stretched a bit—but he brushed it aside impatiently. "You've got to get out of here, Till. Fielder had me followed the other day

45

when I came to see you. Something happened to the two Surety men, but I've got no way of knowing whether they reported back or not—or if he knows I've been coming here. Till, you've got to go back to Betastan."

She laughed at him. "For a member of the Central Comita, you're certainly weak on developments, Rossie. The border's been closed for a week."

"But surely you must have some secret way of getting your agents in and out. Don't tell me there are no Betastan agents in this country besides yourself. From what Fielder and Croft-Gordon report, Alphaland must be swarming with them."

"Yes, but I'm a cloddy when it comes to swimming," she said. "Even with flippers and snorkle."

"Swimming?"

"My sweet Rossie, in this day of radar and warning systems of a double-dozen types, do you think a Betastan agent could sneak across your borders, laden down with cloak and dagger espionage devices? Do you think he could cross the borders in a hopper, or parachute down, even though he started as high up as an artificial satellite? Perish the thought, lover-mine. That military machine Number One and Marshal Croft-Gordon have bled Alphaland white by building, has every last gismo known to the shoot-'em-up boys throughout United Planets. I don't think we could get a carrier pigeon with a metal capsule on his leg across the Marshal's warning system."

He shook his head, scowling. "I suppose you're right, but how *do* your agents get in, then? I know perfectly well they're increasing in number."

She laughed at him again and took up her quiver to sling it over her shoulder. "They swim in from specially designed, wooden, foot-powered, submarines, laddy-buck. Nude. And if the good Coaid Marshal can figure out some way of telling the difference between a

46

man and one of the numerous sea-going mammals of this planet, he's welcome to intercept them."

Suddenly she dropped her bantering tone and stood before him. Her small hands went up to rest on his shoulders.

"Thanks for the warning, Rossie. However, I have reason to believe that Mark Fielder's Surety people still don't know of this place. I'll stick it out for awhile. I've got work to do."

"Till, look. Why don't you marry me? You've spent too many years at this sort of thing, instead of looking into a woman's real place in life. What you need is love, Till. A home, children, a . . . a husband to look after. You've kept your nose to this espionage grindstone too long. You've had no experience in . . . well, in romance, in love. It's time you learned . . ."

She put a finger to his lips.

"When this is over, Rossie, perhaps things will be different." Her face went Chaplinesque. "I'm glad to know you're so up on such matters. Because you're quite right, I've never had much time for such things as romance, Rossie. Someday I'll be glad to have you give me the benefit of your long, hard experience."

V

TILLY TRICE, bow slung over her shoulder, marched smartly up the thirty and more stone steps toward the impressive edifice ahead. Behind her, two by two and in moderately good order, came a full score of similarly garbed, similarly armed seeming youngsters. Surely, the oldest appeared to be no more than eighteen; some, such as Tilly herself, a mere fifteen.

Each carried a quiver of arrows in such a manner that the feathered ends projected over the left shoulder for a quick draw. The bow was slung, almost as though it were a rifle, over the right shoulder. On each head was worn a natty cap, somewhat reminiscent of Robin Hood.

Tilly marched briskly at the fore, a brassard of the Alphaland national colors around her right upper arm, a proud tilt to her head.

The four guards who stood at the top went bug-eyed at the approaching troop—which didn't hesitate for a moment, keeping correct cadence all the way.

At the top, Tilly saluted the Lance Corporal smartly. "Honorary Ensign Lee, reporting for the audience with Deputy Matheison."

He goggled at her blankly.

"Who?" he said. "Now, wait a minute. Who in Zen are you kids? What're you doing here?"

His fellow guards stood in their assigned positions, matching him gape for gape.

Tilly saluted again. "Yes, sir," she said snappily. Bridgetown's Own, First Troop of the Alpha Scouts, reporting for the audience with Deputy Matheison of the Commissariat of Finance."

The Lance Corporal shook his head. "Listen, boy, I never even heard of Bridgetown, let alone the Alpha Scouts. "What're you selling?"

Tilly looked at him reproachfully.

"We're supposed to have an interview and get some sort of engraved plaque for our headquarters."

The corporal looked over his shoulder. "You fellas heard anything about this?"

Two of them shook their heads in utter denial. The other was the type who had to insert himself, whatever.

He said, "Well, Corporal, it seems to me I saw something on the Tri-Di news. Something about the Deputy being going to give some kinds an award, like. Yeah. It seems to me I saw something like that. I could be wrong."

The corporal looked at Tilly in doubt.

"What're those things you got over your backs?"

"We're Alpha Scouts," she said, as though that explained everything.

"Alpha Scouts?" he said dimly.

Tilly said: *"Come wend the wild wi' me,*
　　　　　"Venture shall ever be."

The lance corporal blinked. He bit his under lip.

"We ain't never had no delegates of Alpha Scouts before," he admitted.

Tilly said, "I'll come inside and show you my things, and you can phone the Deputy's office and thty'll tell you all about it, I guess." Her mouth trembled infinitesimally. "They couldn't have forgot about the award," she said miserably. "Not after we came all the way from Bridgetown."

"Okay, kid," the guard said hurriedly. "Come on in."

He had meant only Tilly, but the others filed along behind.

One of the three remaining guards shook his head. "Sooner or later," he said, "you see everything. Hey, you know what those things they was carrying over their backs was? Bows and arrows."

"What's a bows'n'arrows?" one of the others said disinterestedly.

"Don't you ever watch the historic shows on Tri-Di?"

"Naw. I like those burlesque revivals with all the mopsies taking their clothes off all the time."

"Bows and arrows are like the cowboys used to shoot at the Indians. Fella, those were the times. Burning down the wagon trains and rustling the buffalo."

"Wrestling the buffalo?"

An Alpha Scout stuck his head outside the entry and called, "The corporal says for one of you to come in."

One of the guards shrugged and went through the tall opaque door. On the other side, Centurion Combs slapped him behind the ear efficiently with a sap.

Tilly Trice went outside again and said shrilly, "Hey, something's wrong in here. The corporal's sick. He's got some kind of attack."

The remaining two guards made a beeline for the door, the pseudo-knowledgeable one saying, "I always thought he looked like he had a bad ticker, or something."

They pushed on through, their guns comfortably holstered, their minds free of suspicion—and ran into the hands of two so-called Alpha Scouts apiece. They were grabbed efficiently, and Comb's sap thudded once again.

But then with a roar and burst of brawn, the second bashed his two slightly-built assailants together, threw them aside, and was down the corridor, running hard, at the same time tearing at his handgun, opening his mouth to shout a warning.

Tilly called, "Bernal!"

The arrow caught the fleeing guard in the upper spine and he was dead before his body hit the marble flooring.

Tilly snapped, "All right, Combs, Bernal, Altshuler, Zimmerman. You and your men, double time. You know your posts. Take them! Gonzales, stick close to me. Let's go!"

On the run, they sped down corridors that seemed no strangers to them. On the several occasions that they came against Surety guards, or civilian-dressed employees of the Commissariat, the reaction of the others was such that the critical initial seconds of contact were their undoing. The halls were littered with Alphaland citizenry, either battered to insensibility or transfixed with lethal arrows.

Tilly finally stopped. "This is it, isn't it, Manuel?"

"Should be. Let's hurry." The other looked like a kid in no more than his late teens, unless inspection came close enough to take in the wrinkles in his forehead, the depth of intelligence in his eyes. He wore heavy contact lenses. Of them all, he alone seemed nervous, as though the pace of action was unaccustomed.

Tilly whispered urgently, "On your toes, boys. There'll be action here."

She banged her slight shoulder against the massive door.

Beyond, two Surety men were hurrying toward them, one with gun in hand, the other in the process of drawing.

An arrow winged its deadliness past Tilly, missing her by less than six inches. It sped halfway through the lead guard's throat, projecting its bloodiness behind, as the man crumbled forward to his knees, and then, gurgling, flat on his face, his feet drumming agony against the heavy carpeting.

The second guard got one bolt off before being transfixed with three more arrows, then he too went down.

"All right," Tilly said. "Gonzales, it's all yours. Fast now. We'll hold until you're through. But according to your speed, or lack of it, we'll get out of here or not."

Manuel Gonzales unslung a purse-like affair from over his shoulder. He put it down carefully on a heavy table and began hurriedly bringing its contents forth, to lay them in semi-orderly rows on the table. His mouth was dry and he licked his lips often, with little result.

He held an extension cord over his shoulder without looking to see who might take it. "Plug this in," he said, his voice high. He cleared his throat. His hands were flying.

Tilly was standing in the middle of the large room, her bow in hand, an arrow on the string.

Combs, cool as winter wind, came to the assistance of Manuel Gonzales, who was occasionally fumbling his gadgets.

Combs said, soothingly, "How's it work, Manuel?"

Gonzales spoke, even as he tinkered. "It discharges a

condenser-bank through a small coil, generating a very powerful magnetic pulse; then a charge of high explosive is rigged to implode the resultant magnetic field to produce an empire-size flux density. Just a single two-microsecond pulse—but it makes every computer-magnetic-memory within half a mile 'forget' all its information and the data stored in the machine at the time, necessitating complete reprogramming. It also whips most of the magnetic tape around, lousing up records no end."

Admiration in his voice, Combs said, "You lost me somewhere back there, but it sounds swell. We should've tried to get it into the War Ministry."

Tilly, still standing, arrow still on string, said, "No. Finance is even better. You don't fight wars with soldiers anymore, not primarily."

Altshuler came in from the corridor, his face strained. He said, "Zimmerman copped one. That single bolt the guard got off."

Tilly looked at the two technicians. "Try to hurry it, fellows." She went out into the hall.

Several of the so-called Alpha Scouts, their bows at the ready, were standing guard. Two of them were bent over Zimmerman, who was propped up in a sitting position against the wall. His face was unnaturally pale and blood had already soaked through the improvised bandages.

"How bad is it, Zim?" Tilly asked.

"It's pretty bad," he grated. "I'll never make it."

Tilly told those working on him, "When we run for it, you two carry him. The rest of us will cover."

Zimmerman shook his head. "It'd jeopardize everybody. Besides, if they got me, they'd stick me under Scop and I'd betray half our people in town. I'm expendable, Till. Finish me."

Her lips thinned back over her artificial buckteeth. She stared down at him.

Finally she said, "Anything you want passed back home?"

He shook his head again. "No. I said my famous last words when I left to come over here. I knew there was fat chance of ever coming back."

"All right," she said, so low as hardly to be heard. Her eyes went suddenly to Bernal. "It's an order, Bernal!"

An arrow smashed the heart of the fallen guerrilla.

Gonzales and Combs came running from the inner room.

"Let's go!" Combs yelled.

They dashed down the corridors, back the way they had come. Their other groups merged with them as they progressed, coming on the run from the different points to which they had scattered when first entering the building. Three were missing, besides Zimmerman.

They sped out the entry through which they had come a scant ten minutes earlier, and down the stone steps. There were shouts and sounds of confusion behind them, but none bothered to turn head to check the pursuit.

At the bottom of the steps, a supposed tourist hover-bus edged up to the curb, even as they approached. They piled into it—on the surface a gang of teen-agers, costumed as though some sort of club.

Combs was last, almost missing the bus as it took off, being pulled in the door at the last moment by Tilly Trice.

"Thanks," he puffed. "Remind me to marry you some-day. Like your style."

"Tu, tu, tu," she told him. "Already spoken for."

He looked at her sourly. "Oh, too bad."

The bus sped around a corner, barreled at full speed down a boulevard, spun around another corner.

Altshuler, at the rear, called, "Uh-oh, some kind of Surety car."

Tilly yelled back to him, "Noise makes no difference now. Take it!

A moment later a shattering blast tore up the street behind them.

Altshulter looked admiringly down at a small grenade in his hand, the twin of the one he had just thrown. "Zen!" he said. "Ordinance is really turning them out these days."

Tilly clucked. "Watch your patriotism, Alt. Those aren't the products of *our* ordinance plants. They were liberated from a local armory. How d'ya think we'd ever get such equipment over the borders with the kind of security they have here?"

VI

NUMBER ONE was doing his best to relax in the comforting presence of Pater Riggin. He sipped at a glass of amontillado, imported for his sole use from a far land once called Spain.

The Temple Monk said softly, "So the die is cast and there is no return."

Number One shifted in his comfortable chair. "Was there ever a return, Rig?"

"Possibly that's according to where you start from, Jim."

The other shook his heavy head. "There is never return, Rig. No matter how seemingly powerful you are, it's an illusion. You're pushed, you don't march bravely forth."

"I'm not so sure I follow you," the plumpish Temple Monk said. They were seated in the living room of the Presidor's private quarters, as before, an old-fashioned wood fire in the fireplace.

Number One looked at him strangely. "Do you think that Caesar could have changed his mind and *not* crossed the Rubicon?"

Pater Riggin looked at him for a long moment. "You didn't want power, Jim?"

"No. It was thrust upon me. When the collapse of the past regime came, power lay there on the streets for anyone at all to take up. Should I have left it to the Karlists, or some other crackpot group?"

The Temple Monk patted his rounded tummy and said mildly, "I have heard the story before, Jim. 'If I didn't do it, somebody else would.' Also, 'I did it for the sake of others.'"

Number One scowled. "Sometimes I wonder what you really think about me, Rig. And more often I realize I don't want to know. You're the one man I feel I can talk to. But, carrying out along this line, what could I have done otherwise? You know my career as well as I do. Where could I have taken this turning, rather than that one?"

Pater Riggin shook his head. "I doubt if you have ever read of a Yugoslavian named Djilas. However . . ."

"Yugoslavian?"

"A small country in Europe in the old days. During the Second War, it went Communist. Djilas was one of its top revolutionists, the right-hand man of the dictator-to-be, Tito. Djilas spent years in the government prisons, later fought for more years in the mountains as a partisan. When the war was over and his people in power, he was aghast. His comrades were quickly enriching themselves, entrenching themselves in lucrative government jobs for which they were often unsuited. Tito himself lived like an Oriental potentate. When Djilas, still the idealist, refused to conduct himself similarly and attempted to expose this New Class that had arisen from among the supposedly selfless leaders of the proletariat, he was imprisoned for his pains."

"Your point?" the Presidor growled, finishing his wine and reaching for the humidor.

"I'm not sure I have one," his old friend said wryly, "but I find in history few idealists who can resist wealth and power, once they are in grasp. It applies, of course, not only to political figures. Have you ever seen a religion which, once come to acceptance, does not indulge its leadership? My studies tell me most of the great religions were founded by men who foreswore material goods, but, once the religion was established, their following priests were seldom to be found among the poverty-stricken."

Number One looked at him thoughtfully. "I sometimes wonder that the United Temple puts up with you, Rig."

His companion chuckled. "You should be able to figure that out, Jim. I am your closest companion. My immediate Bishop, and his Holiness himself, might occasionally become impatient, but they can't afford to bar from conclave the man who has Number One's ear."

"I've told you I don't like that term," The Presidor growled.

Before the other could answer, a light flickered on the door and the screen there hummed.

Number One glowered at it. "What is this, a shuttle station? I gave orders not to be disturbed. Once this damned war begins, I'll be fortunate to sleep four hours a night."

"Ignore it." Pater Riggin shrugged plump shoulders. "Why do you have deputies?"

The other grunted, pressed a button set into the arm of his chair and came to his feet, scowling, to face the door.

It came open and Jon Matheison, close pressed behind by Mark Fielder, came hurrying through. The former's face was livid with anger—anger and what would seem to be despair.

Number One was curt. "What is the meaning of this intrusion, Coaids? The Crusade is scheduled in a few days. I have need of time for rest and contemplation."

His Deputy of Finance began to say something, but Mark Fielder cut in, even as his eyes shifted about the apartment, taking in this, taking in that, resting briefly on Pater Riggin.

The Surety man said, "The war, evidently, is already on."

"What! You mean they've attacked first!"

Matheison said, "An unprovoked attack on my commissariat. I have still not completely evaluated the disaster."

Number One was glaring. "Make sense, you two! What has happened?"

His financial head took a deep breath. "As far as we can make out, a group of a hundred or more Betastani, armed with bows and arrows, broke into the Treasury Building this afternoon. They. . . ."

"Armed with *what?*"

"Bows and arrows," Fielder said grimly. "Their value as a secret weapon applies not only to this romp. The damned things don't make a sound, produce no muzzle-flash, don't affect capacitance-alarm circuits so they can be back-trajectoried to locate their source. They ring no alarms, since they're of wood rather than metal. The funkers even had hard plastic arrowheads on the nardy things."

"The Treasury!" Pater Riggin blurted. "Why the Treasury? You mean they made off with . . ."

Matheison shot a contemptuous look at him. "Gold? No, of course not. Even if there had been a good many more of them they couldn't have taken off enough gold to make any difference, and even that's if they could have gotten down into the vaults, which would have been impossible."

"Then what *did* they do?" Number One rasped.

Uninvited, the Deputy of Finance sank down onto a couch. He shook his head unbelievingly. "They used some sort of device I didn't even know could exist. I don't know how it works. I don't really know what they did. But all out data banks are scrambled. Scrambled, I tell you. We have nothing. Nothing we can depend on."

Number One felt a certain relief. He hadn't known what sort of emergency, what tragedy to the Alphaland cause, had been brought before him. This seemed comparatively picayune.

He went over to the bar and poured a drink, brought it back and handed it to his visitor. "Drink this," he growled. "You're upset." He switched his eyes to his Deputy of Surety. "Just what happened? You two don't make much sense."

"The details aren't in," Fielder said, his voice returning to its usual suavity. "However, it would seem that a large body of Betastani agents, carrying weapons deliberately designed not to affect our Surety alarms, invaded Coaid Matheison's offices in the records wing of Finance."

"Are government offices that vulnerable?"

Fielder made a gesture of helplessness with manicured hands. "One wouldn't expect an attack to take place at such a point. The romp was unprecedented in any case, but the last locale one would expect would be the innocuous records offices of the Finance Commissariat."

"Go on!"

"They killed several of the few guards who are posted at Finance, and then set up a device that has wiped every memory tape within blocks."

"Did you catch any of them?"

Fielder shook his head, his expression empty. "They must have been highly picked men. Dedicated. They" —he hesitated—"they finished off their own wounded."

A look of distaste went over Pater Riggin's face.

Number One came back to his finance chief. "All right, what does it mean? What difference does it make? Why'd they bother to go to the trouble?"

Matheison stared at him as though unbelieving. "What difference does it make?" For once his indignation overrode his awe of his leader. "But they were the banks of all our records. There are no others."

"Bring it down to a layman's understanding, and cut out all this jetsam!" Number One growled.

Matheison took a deep breath. "Your Leadership, the Alphaland monetary system is based on the gold Alpha. In ancient times when a coinage system was first hit upon on Mother Earth—in Lydia, Asia Minor, to be exact, about 700 B.C.—it was very simple. The coinage, both gold and silver, was literally worth the weight of the precious metal involved. Even when paper money evolved, the bills were backed by gold, or silver. Thus a person holding a piece of paper money could go to the treasury that had issued it and demand the amount of gold."

"I am not a schoolboy," Number One rumbled. "Get to the point."

"Your Leadership, as matters financial became more elaborate what with a burgeoning commerce, international trade, and so forth, we ceased dealing, more and more, with gold or silver itself and most transactions took place on paper. But always with the gold in the background; buried away in vaults, but always ultimately backing banking transactions. Centuries ago, the credit card began to evolve, slowly at first, but with growing speed as business machines, computers and data-processing developed. And now, today, actual coinage is practically unknown. Even an employee is not paid directly now. His salary automatically goes into his account. When he spends money, he simply presents his universal credit card, and the sum is deducted from the proper account."

The Presidor's eyes began to widen.

"Everything, but *everything*, is handled by our computers and their auxiliaries. In actuality, only some fifteen percent of Alphaland's currency is backed by the gold in our vaults, but that has been deemed enough. If a foreign nation finds itself holding a considerable credit of Alphas, it can demand, and receive, the amount in gold bullion. But don't you see what has happened? The magnitude of it? There were no records whatsoever except those we kept in our data banks. A common yoke who had savings of no more than five Alphas to his credit now has no record to prove it; the wealthiest banker with credits of a hundred million Alphas is in the same position. Nobody has any record."

"What it amounts to," Mark Fielder broke in with, "is that these Betastan criminals have robbed the nation of endless billions of gold Alphas. At the present time, for all practical purposes, every citizen in Alphaland is bankrupt!"

"That's not exactly the way I'd put it," Matheison said weakly.

Marshal Croft-Gordon, in full rage, stormed into the room without announcing himself.

"What in the name of Zen is all this! How can you prosecute a war without funds! We're no longer in an age when the citizenry simply grab up their own swords and spears and dash out to confront the enemy! My forces expend half a billion a week just remaining at peace! What is this?"

Number One didn't remember to glare at the cavalier intrusion.

It was Pater Riggen who ejaculated, "Holy Ultimate!"

They stood before the charts in Number One's secret command post.

Number One said grimly, checking his wrist chronom-Croft-Gordon. Deputer Mark Fielder of the Commissariat of Surety. Temple Bishop Stockwater. Academecian Philip McGivern of the Department of Socioeconomics. Deputy Jon Matheison of Finance. Ross Westley of the Commissariat of Information. All except the last being the inmost associates of the Presidor of the Free Democratic Commonwealth of Alphaland.

Number One said grimly, checking his wrist chronoeter, "Very well, the ultimatum has been issued. I assume, Marshal, that your forces are ready to move."

Marshal Croft-Gordon cracked his swagger stick against his leg. "And have been for two months. My own opinion is that this ultimatum is a mistake. We should have struck as I suggested in my original plans, based on the first computer results."

Number One looked at him expressionlessly. "Nobody asked for your own opinion, Marshal. Please bear in mind that the ultimate command of the Alphaland military is in the hands of the Presidor. This seems increasingly to escape you, Marshal."

"Yes, Your Leadership," the Marshal said stiffly.

Number One said as an afterthought, "Coaid Fielder, I assume you have taken the precaution of rounding up all nationals of Betastan."

For the moment, the Surety Deputy said nothing and all eyes went to him.

"Well?" his leader growled.

"Your Leadership, it has been obvious for some time that the war was inevitable. For that reason, undoubtedly, a large number of enemy aliens have long since departed. When my men took the obvious steps of arresting those remaining, they found only a handful of elderly people and a few score of infants."

The United Temple representative to the Central

61

Comita said in complete surprise, "But, my son, there are thousands of Betastani resident in this city alone."

Mark Fielder looked at the Temple Bishop. "There were, but no longer."

The aged Philip McGivern rubbed his graying goatee and muttered impatiently, "Without doubt, the majority have fled to the countryside in anticipation of Betastan bombing."

Marshal Croft-Gordon said, "There'll be no enemy bombing of Alphacity. They'll never get through our border defenses, not to speak of those of the city."

Fielder said easily, "At any rate, those of the enemy nationals still in Alphaland will be seized soon enough. They can't hide for any appreciable time. Among other things, the patriotism of our own civilians will prevent them from keeping under cover."

"I hope you're right," Ross said.

Number One looked at him bleakly. "Clarify that, Coaid!"

Ross said doggedly, "I warned you that a month was insufficient time to prepare our people for a war of aggression."

"War of aggression?" Temple Bishop Stockwater protested. "My son, your term is most distressing. This Crusade against the ungodly is to *repel* aggression and come to the aid of those who would throw off the bonds of the evil Amish-Karlist regime that now subverts the freedom of the Betastani people."

Ross said, "We've dropped that Amish bit, Your Blessedness. Or, at least, we're phasing it out as rapidly as we can."

"But these Amish are nonbelievers," the Temple Bishop said in indignation.

Number One rumbled, "Let's stop all this jetsam!" He looked at his chronometer. "Ten minutes to go." He turned to his military chief. "You are confident of complete destruction of the primary targets?"

Marshal Croft-Gordon blew out his cheeks. "The computers indicate a three time overkill. The ten most populous cities, including the capital, New Betatown. The ten largest industrial complexes. The forty largest airports, both military and civilian. All military bases with a personnel of more than one thousand."

"I am aware of the targets," Number One rumbled. "But are you positive of complete destruction?"

"A three time overkill, Your Leadership."

The aged Academecian McGivern said musingly, "It will provide an excellent basis for their economy of the future. A pastoral economy. We should never, Your Leadership, allow them to recover from this destruction of both their cities and industrial complexes. Our own population centers, so our good Marshal assures us, will remain untouched by what remaining aircraft and missiles they might possess. In the future, we will supply what manufactured products the Betastani need."

There was a humming of the door and an aide went to check it.

He returned with a confused looking colonel who snapped to attention upon confronting the Marshal of the Armies. "Sir, a report."

Number One growled, "You will render your report directly to me, Captain."

The newcomer looked at him, startled. "Uh, it's Colonel, Your Leadership."

"Your mistake. From now on, it's Captain. In the future, I suggest that in my presence you address me first, not one of my Coaids, Captain."

"Yes, Your Leadership."

"Now, what's your damned message? It had better be important."

"Your Leadership, there has been a response to your ultimatum. In fact, the response is being broadcast by every means from the Betastani to the whole planet."

"A response? So soon? Impossible!"

Number One darted a glare at his Marshal. "Are the missiles and bombers on their way?"

"No, Your Leadership. We had another five or six minutes to go." The Marshal looked blank. He shot a look at the military charts on the walls. The points marked in red were to have been struck. He banged his uniform leg with his swagger stick in irritation.

Number One turned his glare back to the ex-colonel, now captain.

"What kind of response, confound it?"

The captain brought up a military report. "Your Leadership, they have declared their ten largest population centers open cities. Each of these cities has surrendered to you."

"Surrendered!" the Marshal barked. "We haven't even landed a single man!"

"Silence!" Number One said curtly. He turned his rage on the captain. "What else? I can see there is something else!"

"Your Leadership, a whole series of industrial complexes—industries, mills, mines—have also surrendered. Declared themselves open areas, the equivalent of open cities."

"You mean the Betastan government has surrendered?" Number One demanded unbelievingly.

"Praise to the Holy Ultimate," The Temple Bishop intoned reverently.

"Shut up, confound it!"

The captain swallowed. "No, sir. That doesn't seem to be it. It's just these individual cities and industrial complexes have declared themselves open and have surrendered. They're awaiting your occupation forces, Your Leadership. All military units have been withdrawn into the countryside."

Number One, for once, was uncomprehending. For a moment it looked as though he were about to lapse into one of his characteristic moods of contemplation, but then he tossed his heavy head abruptly. He turned to Marshal Croft-Gordon and Deputy Fielder.

"Your opinions, Coaids?"

Croft-Gordon bit out, "Send the bombers! This is a trick. Level them!"

Ross Westley, with formerly unknown vigor snapped, "No! Didn't you hear this man? The Betastani have broadcast their surrender to the whole planet. Not a person of good will, not only in the neutral countries but in Alphaland itself, would stand for an attack upon those cities now!"

"All the largest cities have surrendered?" McGivern said in shocked tones. "Why, the computers said the war would be over in less than three months, but at this rate, they won't last three weeks."

"At this rate, they won't last three days," Mark Fielder amended. "There's something awfully wrong, here. I don't like it."

PART TWO

VII

NUMBER ONE, surrounded by his inmost staff, had fallen into deep thought. Not a breath could have been heard. Even the colonel who had brought the announcement of the surrender of Betastan's largest centers, although he had never been in the presence of his ultimate superior before, knew the story of the Presidor's lapses into contemplation and the fate of any who interrupted such a reverie.

But Marshal of the Armies Rupert Croft-Gordon could stand it no longer.

"We've got to act!" he barked.

Number One's eyes came away from far distances. He regarded his military chief desolately. "Very well, Coaid, order the advance. Our armies are to counter the provocations of the Betastani border aggressions. They are to return force with force, in the defense of the Motherland and the Holy United Temple."

"The cities?" the Marshal demanded. "Shall we strike the cities?"

"No. All air fleets and missiles are to be reassigned targets of secondary importance. The secondary targets they would have hit upon leveling these that have declared themselves open."

"But it's a trick! Our whole campaign is based upon the destruction of those primary targets."

Number One nodded grimly. "I suspect you are correct. This then shall be our procedure: air marines shall land in light force in New Betatown and all the other so-called open cities and industrial areas."

"In light force?" Mark Fielder protested. "They wouldn't last the day out."

The Presidor nodded again. "That is my suspicion, Coaid. And this is my declaration: in any city, or other locale, which has declared itself open, if a single Alphaland trooper is killed, then the city's classification is voided and our missiles will immediately retaliate."

Ross Westley said, shock in his voice, "You mean that each detachment of our own air marines is to be considered expendable? That if any action takes place in any of these cities, the place would be leveled, which would automatically eliminate our occupying force there as well?"

Number one didn't bother to answer.

Temple Bishop Stockwater intoned, "Such sons of the Motherland and of the United Temple will proudly offer their lives to the Crusade."

Ross shot an indignant look at him.

The Marshal said, "I'll issue immediate orders to occupy the points in question." He moved over to a visiophone.

After a few moments, he touched a stud to amplify. Over the communication device could be heard, although over a great distance, the sounds of artillery and bombs.

"The counterattack is launched!" the Marshal proclaimed.

Number One looked at his assistants, one by one, his face expressionless. "Very well, Coaids, the die is cast. It is now in the hands of the Holy Ultimate."

The Temple Bishop bowed his head. "Amen."

Ross Westley, his face glum, wove his way through the chaos of his outer offices. The Commissariat of Information was in full swing, in full voice. Clerks ran rather than walked; every office machine in the series of rooms seemed in full clatter. All was monstrous confusion.

He snorted.

Ross sometimes wondered what was transpiring in this, his own department, and realized that he, as supposed head of it all, had only a glimmering of understanding. The Commissariat of Information. Under one department or the other, it either originated, or censured, every book, every article, every fictional piece, every show—legitimate, Tri-Di, or tape. Not even nightspot comedians were free of the ever-present scrutiny of his minions, and woe to him whose sly innuendo touched upon matters political or religious or dwelt, even in far passing, upon the prerogatives of the Presidor or of the United Temple.

But Ross himself? He suspected that if he should secretly drop dead months would go by before anyone in his million-tentacled organization would realize it; that not a computer, not a collator, not a sorter or keypunch would slow even momentarily.

He snorted.

Sometimes he suspected that the same applied to every

bureaucrat on every level. He himself dealt with his immediate assistant, Job Bauserman, and such department heads as Martha Taylor and Pater Ian, and seldom with anyone below that level. He hardly even knew the names of any of the lower assistants.

But take Number One. He also dealt with his immediate Coaids, his deputies. And he probably didn't know the names of any under that level. And suppose the Presidor suddenly decided to withdraw into his own apartments for a week, a month, a year. Would the workings of the bureaucracy stop? Hardly.

He grunted contempt. The historian in him wondered. Would the Macedonian armies have continued on and conquered Persia had Alexander been killed at Issus? He suspected they would have. The Greek star was in the ascendancy, the Persian on the decline. Had Napoleon died in Egypt, would the exploding, idealistic people's armies of the French have conquered Europe? Why not? It was in the cards that feudalistic Austria and the German and Italian states couldn't stand against the new socioeconomic forces. Would the fate of Europe been greatly different had Hitler died in the streets of Munich during his first putsch? Probably not. Germany was fated to make her bid for control of Europe, and with the British Commonwealth, the Soviet goliath and industrially overwhelming America against her, fated to lose.

Somebody had said something to him. He scowled and halted.

"I beg your pardon."

It was one of his senior secretaries, stationed immediately outside his office. What was her confounded name? Yes, Jet Pirincin.

"Coaid Westley. A new report has just come in. Our glorious armies are everywhere victorious. They have pressed an average of more than twenty miles across the borders of the aggressor."

"Let me see it," he muttered, halting at her desk. "The

computers didn't figure on an advance quite that fast."

She held out a portable scanner for him.

He grunted. "Everywhere victorious?" he asked sarcastically. "They haven't even come in contact with the enemy yet."

"The funkers are in full retreat," she said. "Even their navy. It all remains submerged, afraid to come to blows with our ships."

Ross looked at her. "See these reports get on my desk." He handed back the scanner and headed again for his office.

He tried to remember the figures on the size of the Betastani navy. As he recalled, it was on the smallish side and consisted almost entirely of lighter craft. Possibly the girl was right and the enemy ships were afraid to come to blows with their heavier Alphaland opponents.

Martha Taylor was waiting in his inner quarters. She sat primly on the edge of the most uncomfortable chair in the room, a lettercase in her lap.

He took his own chair and said wearily, "Coaid Taylor?"

She stood and put the folder before him.

"The atrocity releases," she said.

"The what?"

"The atrocities," she told him. "Four of them, so far. Mobs of uncontrolled slum elements in New Betatown roaming the streets, breaking into the houses of citizens of Alphaland and destroying their furniture, burning their possessions, beating them sometimes to death, all while Betastani police look on laughing."

"Holy Jumping Zen!" he blurted. "How do you know? How could you get such a report?"

It was her turn to look blank. She said, "Assistant Deputy Bauserman himself wrote it up."

He shook his head, realizing that he hadn't been concentrating. This was, after all, the department of propaganda. He was comparatively new to the job, but he wasn't that naïve.

"What else?" he said.

She put a paper before him. "Two Temple Monks crucified and their Temple burned to the ground. Three Nuns hospitalized after being raped."

He closed his eyes briefly at that one.

"What else?"

"The President of Betastan has issued orders that his armies take no prisoners of war."

"That's going to be refuted awfully quickly. They have access to the airwaves, too. Besides, President Alf Mortiary is internationally known as a bumbling, easygoing old figurehead—not as a fire-eater who orders prisoners shot."

Her dried out, sexless face expressed doubt. "Perhaps we could report him fleeing the country for sanctuary in Moravia. Then we could hang the Karlist label on him that much more strongly, since Moravia is now in the hands of the Karlists."

Ross looked up at her. "Listen, here in my own office, let's stick to reality."

"I beg your pardon, Coaid Deputy?"

"The Karlists aren't in control of Moravia, and you know it. And you also know that old Mortiary isn't a Karlist. He doesn't have enough brains to be a Karlist."

Martha Taylor did a double take. "Why, Coaid . . ."

"What's the fourth release?" he asked wearily.

"Betastani civilians, resident here in Alphaland, are blowing up bridges, destroying communication lines, cutting pnueumatic pressure lines."

"Oh, now, that's *too* raw. Remember, this material goes out all over the planet. No neutral is going to swallow that."

She was wide-eyed. "But, Coaid, that's the one that's really true."

"What?"

70

She held up another report. "Evidently bands of them are all over the countryside. Deputy Fielder has ordered out over half his Surety men. Thousands of Betastani nationals have taken to our woods, the mountains, and are committing endless depredations."

"Holy Jumping Zen," Ross muttered. "Tilly."

"I beg your pardon?"

"Nothing," he said. "Listen, take all this to Coaid Bauserman and tell him I said to use his discretion."

"Yes, Coaid Deputy."

"And don't bother me with such stuff in the future. It's strictly routine anyway, isn't it?"

"Well," she seemed upset. "I suppose so, Coaid Deputy."

"All right, toss it into Bauserman's lap. It had a tendency to nauseate me."

When she was gone, after flashing her shock at him, he realized he had gone too far. Well, the hell with it. He realized, too, that he disliked the presence of Coaid Martha Taylor, that she made him nervous.

He switched on his orderbox and said into it. "Rundown of latest dispatches. Verbal."

The orderbox said, *"The government of the archcriminal Alf Mortiary has deserted the capital, New Betatown, and its present location is unknown. Rumors are that it is fleeing the country."*

Ross grunted. That was surprisingly similar to the propaganda release Martha Taylor had just recommended.

The report continued. *"Contact between the glorious avenging armies of Alphaland and the retreating Betastan forces has yet to be made. Our armies are at some points now fifty miles into the interior. Advance elements are slowing, to allow supply columns to come up and to repair roads, bridges and communications lines destroyed by the retreating enemy. Alphaland air units have complete control of the skies. Enemy aircraft have as yet been uncommitted.*

"On the home front, Deputy John Matheison of the Commissariat of Finance has announced that his organization is working around the clock reestablishing order in the medium of exchange. He has warned unpatriotic elements that taking advantage of the present credit situation can lead to legal prosecution, and, since the nation is at war defending itself against the aggressors of Betastan, the death penalty can be suffered."

Ross Westley hissed surprise through his teeth. Jon Matheison must have his troubles indeed, to get that tough. Evidently many a less than loyal citizen of Alphaland was taking advantage of the chaos to enrich himself. Ross was almost amused. It was going to be all but impossible to apprehend any such opportunists. Business was in such a state of unbelievable confusion that he wondered at Number One's decision to get the war under way before the financial mess had been cleaned up.

He said into the orderbox, "That will be all," and then slumped back and stared at it. He shifted in his chair, uncomfortably, unhappily. And suddenly he came to his feet. He couldn't put it off any longer. He had to try and find out what had happened to her.

Ross Westley strode quickly toward the closet-like receptacle of his one-seated private pneumatic.

There was a Surety man in riot police uniform, standing before the bookshop which had been the front for Tilly Trice. When Ross came up the brawny agent looked at him scowlingly.

"Move along, Coaid," he said.

Ross Westley considered for a moment, but the urge was upon him. He brought forth his wallet and showed the other his credentials. The Surety man snapped to attention, eyes forward.

"Yes, Coaid Deputy."

Ross said, "What're you doing here, Coaid?"

"Yes, Coaid Deputy. This is the former business and

residence of a Betastani national. I have been posted to guard it against neighborhood reprisal, until a thorough search of the premises can be made."

Ross nodded. "I see. Protection against demonstrators, eh?"

"Yes, Coaid Deputy. Only it seems that this Tilly Trice was kinda popular around the neighborhood, even if she was a Betastani cloddy. So not even the kids've thrown any rocks or anything. They don't need me here."

Ross winked at him. "Well, I'm glad I arrived before the search squad. I hope you have the key, Coaid."

The Surety man showed his surprise. "Yes, Coaid Deputy. Uh, why?"

Ross winked again. "This enemy shop used to sell ancient first edition books, that sort of thing. I'm a collector. I'd like to, ah, take a look around before the place is ransacked. By the way, give me your name—I like a cooperative man. Never know when I might be able to do you a favor."

Three minutes later he was in the shop where a hundred times over he had been with the girl he loved. He closed the door behind him.

His eyes went over the shelves of books. In actuality, he wasn't particularly interested in the old style books of paper; Tilly's own interest, however, had been genuine and it was all part of her. On her worktable sat a half assembled volume which he remembered she had been rebinding, glue pot and leather scraps to one side. He wondered vaguely what the interruption had been.

Had Surety agents knocked on the front door, sending her scurrying out the rear? Had she heard radio reports and headed for some secret hideaway? He couldn't imagine her giving up the fray. Somewhere in Alphaland the diminutive Tilly Trice was still holding forth. He suspected that she was among those guerrillas causing trouble to the transport and communications systems. It might be weeks before all of them were rounded up. He felt the cold go through him. Mark Fielder's heavies weren't going to be particularly gentle with the saboteurs. She could well be hurt, if not killed, in the skirmishing that was sure to ensue.

He looked around the little shop, knowing that whatever happened it could never ,be the same again. And he wondered why he had to come. To see if he could find some indication of where she might be? Hardly probable. Tilly Trice, Betastan espionage agent, was not so inept as to leave a clue for Surety men to follow up.

He walked back toward her living quarters in the rear. There were, he knew, her tiny living room, her still smaller bedroom, an auto-chef table in a dinette, and, of course, a refresher room. All very compact. All very much the home of a feminine bachelor.

He picked up an object here, one there, with which he affiliated her. A book she had evidently been reading, before she had gone on the run.

Ross looked at the title and winced. *Guerrilla Warfare*, by Ho Chi Minh.

He tossed the book back to the side table and wandered vaguely back into her bedroom. There was a feeling of empty apathy in him. He stood there, eyeing her comparatively Spartan dressing table. He walked to her closet and opened the door, having in mind looking at her dresses, her suits—not exactly knowing why. And was confronted with a slightly built, youthful-faced man who held at the easy ready a very efficient looking handgun trained on Ross Westley's belly.

Had the other been a winged angel with a triple set of halos, Ross Westley couldn't have been more taken aback. He gaped at the gunman.

The newcomer, not moving, his gun hand not shifting the aim one iota, looked at Ross with a surly expression.

74

"I'm afraid we're not very well met, fella," he said.

Ross blurted, "What. . . . what . . . ?"

"You said a mouthful, fella. Come along inside. You showed up at exactly the wrong time for your own good."

"Inside?" Ross said blankly. He looked over his shoulder. But he had closed the door between the shop and these, Tilly's living quarters, and even had it been open, the Surety man outside could not have seen to this point.

The occupant of the rather large closet made a motion with the gun. "In here, fella, with me. Just the two of us. Real chummy." His face went cold. "Quick!"

Ross came forward, pressing into the hanging clothing, thinking the other mad. What could the possible reason be for entering the hiding place of the stranger?

He felt the gun grind into his belly, felt the other reach past him to close the door. They were instantly in darkness.

And then he gasped as the floor began to sink. It accelerated, elevator-wise, for a brief moment, then came to a halt.

The door opened again and once more Ross gasped.

It was a large, long room of cement, as devoid of decoration as a garage. It had a military aspect, something like a defensive bunker. There were beds in tiers; there were mess hall type tables. And there were weapons of half a dozen types which Ross Westley recognized, and almost as many that he didn't. There seemed to be a good many gadgets of the portable type around, but almost all of these, too, were unfamiliar.

From the bunks where they lay, from the chairs where they sprawled, from around the tables where they played cards or battle chess, a full score of young men looked up at the entry of Ross and his captor.

They were young men and he had the feeling that they looked even younger than they were. In fact, standing immediately beside the gunman he had found in the closet, he realized the other had undergone cosmetic surgery. He hadn't the vaguest idea why.

Somebody chuckled from the bunk. "Well, well, Combs has brought us a new playmate. Great. I was getting sick and tired of you yokes."

Yes, there was at least a full score of them, Ross decided. His mind was only beginning to realize the significance of this.

Those in bed swung their legs about and came erect, the card and battle chess games came to an end and all crowded around the newcomers.

"Where'd you get him, Centurion?" one of them said.

Another poked a finger in Ross' stomach. "Flabby," he said. "Alphaland bureaucrat. Why do all bureaucrats get flabby? You can tell a bureaucrat by his tummy."

Combs said, "Take it easy. I think I know who this one is. I've seen his face on Tri-Di propaganda blasts. We've hit the big bell."

Another voice said from behind him, "All right, fellas, knock it off. What've we got here?"

The voice was happily familiar. The ranks parted but Ross already knew who he was going to see.

"Till!" he said.

She looked at him, hands on slim hips, and shook her head, some of the old mockery there.

Combs said, "I was going up to check the street and ran into him prowling your rooms."

"Why, Rossie!"

He flushed irritation. "I was looking for some clue to where you had gone." He looked around at the rest of them, now flanking her on both sides. "Are you all drivel-happy, hiding here? Do you realize there's a Surety agent stationed out front and that as soon as Mark Fielder's men get around to it, they'll tear this place apart looking for clues?"

She grinned at him. "I rather doubt it, Rossie. Oh, I don't mean they won't tear the shop apart, stealing what they want and vandalizing most of the rest. But they'll do a halfhearted job and finally call it quits, padlock the place and go on to the next former residence of a Betastani, hoping for more lucrative loot. Not in a dozen years, unless they suspected it was there to find, would they spot the closet-elevator arrangement.

"It's an old, old wheeze, Rossie. The safest place to hide something is right under the eyes of the searcher. The *Purloined Letter* bit. Can you think of anywhere in Alphacity where the Surety boys would be less likely to look for me than right here in my own house?"

He shook his head in wonder at her gall, then he looked around at the others accusingly. "You're all spies."

The smiling one who had commented earlier on his flabby stomach grinned. "Not exactly, old fella. We're more like guerrillas, eh? See, we're in uniform. Naughty, naughty, if old Deputy Fielder's men caught us and tried to line us up before a firing squad. Against all the rules of war."

"You call that a uniform?" Ross snorted. "You look like boy scouts."

"That's the way we're supposed to look, fella," another one laughed.

Ross was getting tired of this. Besides, he had found Tilly now; he wanted to make sure of her safety.

He said, "You'd all better consider yourselves under arrest and in my custody. I'll see you get honorable treatment."

The one who had originally captured him grunted surly amusement. "Fella, you've sure got it wrong." He looked at Tilly and said, deadly serious now, "We'll have to crisp him, he's seen too much."

Tilly shook her head. "Impossible," she said, her voice tart.

Somebody else frowned. "There's no alternative. He's seen the place. There's no way of shutting him up otherwise. And there's no way we can keep him under wraps here indefinitely."

Tilly still shook her head. "Even if the rest of it were okay, you're not thinking it out. That Surety man up above saw him come in. He's going to begin wondering, and fairly soon, why he doesn't come out again. So . . . he's got to come out."

"But he'll put the blast on us the moment he's free!"

Tilly shook her head, her mouth pursed in a rueful smile. "No, he won't. You see, I think I'm going to marry the big cloddy when all this is over."

That silenced them, especially Combs.

Ross said urgently, "Listen, Till, come with me. The war's all but over, anyway. There isn't anything more you can do. And as things are you're running one devil of a risk. Your people are committing criminal acts all over the countryside. Mark Fielder's going to get tough. His men are bad, Till. Call it quits now. I keep telling you the war's over."

Combs said grimly, "To the contrary, fella. It hasn't hardly started."

Ross swirled on him. "Hasn't started! Your largest cities have capitulated. Your navy refuses to show its face. Your army is retreating so fast we can't catch up with it. Our computers, reprogrammed to handle the new factors, say the complete collapse of your government will take place within the week." He snorted. "What do your computers say?"

Combs said, "We haven't consulted them, fella."

"No more time," Tilly said, "Altshuler, take him up above—one moment. Rossie, look at me."

He looked into her face, distressed.

She put her hands on his shoulders, then stood quickly on tiptoe and kissed him quickly on the mouth.

She said, "It won't be over as fast and neat as you think, but it'll be over. Don't worry about me. Nothing

78

happens to guerrillas. They work on the principle that it's a mistake to get hurt in a war."

She pushed him toward the closet cum elevator.

When he was gone, she turned back to her score of Betastani irregulars.

Combs said, "Was that good tactics? He's a full deputy in Number One's government. We had him. We could have finished him, and then have gone up and disposed of the Surety man in some manner that would have been believable."

She looked at him perkily. "Tu, tu, tu, Centurion, you continually forget who makes the decisions here. That man we just let get away is going to be one of the levers which overthrows the government of the Free Democratic Commonwealth of Alphaland. That's a revolutionist in embryo that we've got to nourish."

VIII

NUMBER ONE, for once showing his years, sat in almost continual audience consulting with his inmost associates, his deputies of commissariats, and closest advisers. To his side, and slightly behind, was Pater Riggin, largely silent but ever alert. It was more or less unprecedented; the Temple Monk was seldom seen in company with the Presidor, certainly not during official business.

On this occasion, Marshal Croft-Gordon was reporting. His tone of voice was barely short of accusation, as though it were the fault of the Presidor that so much of the unexpected had developed.

"Largely," he rapped, "they retreat. However, in some localities they turn and fight like madmen."

"What localities?"

"Largely, where natural conditions are such that it is

most difficult for us to bring to bear our superior equipment. The Tatra Mountains, for instance, possibly the most rugged on the planet. They evidently have special mountain troops, long trained. The terrain is impossible for tanks, even the light hover models. Aircraft are all but useless, even hoppers. Bombings, although we continue to utilize them, are largely farce and more for the morale of our own troops than for the damage they inflict. Even so, among the peaks, cliffs, gorges, valleys, we've taken a good many aircraft losses when our fliers go in low enough to drop their bombs with any accuracy at all."

Number One scowled at him. "Can't our own men go in on foot?"

"Yes, Your Leadership . . ."

Pater Riggin looked at the military head inquiringly. He hadn't missed the way the other pronounced the title. Evidently, Number One, in his agitation, had failed to notice.

". . . however, mountains in Alphaland are comparatively gentle and our mountaineers few. The Betastani get about on skis and on devices called snowshoes. They have little motorized equipment, but this is especially adapted to snow and mountains. It is as though their commanding officers always expected to fight a defensive action in this terrain. Their men are armed largely with rifles with telescopic sights. Individuals, or small squads, sit in caves or on mountain tops and pick off our men at great distances, one by one. By the time we've secured one area, they manage to infiltrate around it and attack our supply and communications lines from the rear. It is all we can do to program our portable military computers quickly enough to handle each new situation that develops."

Number One thought about it for a time. "Where else do they hold out?"

"In the swampy areas of their southernmost provinces.

It's not quite as bad as the mountains. Some of our equipment is usable, especially along the roads. However . . ." He hesitated. The anger had been growing in his voice as he reported.

"However, what?"

"They blow the bridges, tear down communication lines, destroy surprisingly long stretches of roads going through the worst of the swamp areas." He said, with considerable disgust, "You'd think they didn't give a damn what their countryside will look like when the war is over."

"Scorched earth policy," Pater Riggin muttered.

Number One turned on him. "What?"

The Temple Monk shrugged and patted his rounded tummy. "Back in the early days on Earth, it was occasionally utilized. The Russians, when invaded by Napoleon in command of the most powerful army the world had ever seen, simply continued to fade back before him as he advanced. They destroyed everything in his path, cities, towns, granaries, crops, orchards, all livestock they couldn't drive away. They destroyed, totally, their own country which he was due to overrun. By the time he reached Moscow, supposedly the goal which would mean his victory, his troops were already on short rations. It was before the day of canned food, and his general staff had planned largely to live off the countryside. It is estimated that not one man out of twenty of the Grand Army got back to Europe proper."

Number One felt a twinge go through him. He turned back to Marshal Croft-Gordon. "Go on, Coaid. What else?"

"Largely, we progress elsewhere, with the funkers fleeing before us, unwilling to stand and fight."

"Surely you must be able to corner or surround some elements."

"Of course! You think my army's composed of cloddies?" The Marshal's tone was unnaturally belligerent before his superior. "But when we do, large numbers simply melt away. They dissolve into smaller units and take to the woods, hills, swamps, wherever motorized military units find it most difficult to operate. They become guerrillas, never standing and fighting, but sniping, burning, assassinating. It's the most idiotic, infuriating type of warfare imaginable. Why, there are no back areas. The territory we overrun is never secure. Soldiers on leave, expecting to have a cold glass of guzzle in some local inn, never know when a grenade will be tossed through the window. Soldiers strolling the streets in a conquered village never know when a sniper will pick one off."

Number One fell into thought.

Not even Marshal Croft-Gordon felt rebellious enough to interrupt.

Finally the Presidor shook himself and said, "Would it be of benefit to ignore public opinion and resort to nuclear weapons?"

Both the Marshal and Pater Riggin stared at him in shock.

"*Jim*," the Temple Monk said, so low as hardly to be heard.

The Marshal shook his head in bitter regret. "There are no particular targets we could use. We can't flatten the Tatra Mountains—they cover an area larger than most of the neutral nations can boast. And besides, how can we know what action United Planets might ultimately take? Fusion and even fission weapons have been used only two or three times in the past century among the some three thousand member planets of UP, and in each case it meant disaster for the user."

Number One changed the subject abruptly. "How much of their countryside do we now nominally control?"

"*Nominally* is correct. But including the open cities that capitulated, more than one-half. However, there is another element here. I need more troops. More age groups must be called up to the colors. My men are

being spread too thin, considering the number of guerrillas operating behind our lines."

His ultimate leader nodded wearily. "We'll consider it.
The finances involved are a problem; Coaid Matheison
is still working in a madhouse. So are the anti-draft and
peace riots a problem. But I'll take it up."

Marshal Croft-Gordon barked, "It's not just a matter
of taking it up, Your Leadership. I *must* have more
men, more equipment, more munitions. Do you realize
that the computers estimate that it is taking an average of
fourteen tons of ammunition, bombs or other expendable
material, to kill one Betastani, the way they are now
fighting?"

Number One looked at him bleakly. "Pay attention
to the manner in which you address me, Coaid. I weary
of your lack of courtesy."

*A young woman pushing a baby carriage passed two
Surety guards who idled at a street corner.*

*One of them grinned down into the conveyance, but
she whispered, "Shhhhh, asleep."*

"I gotta little girl," he whispered back.

*She went on her way, turning a corner. The street
was clear before her.*

*She darted her eyes, up, down, then temporarily
abandoned the carriage at an alley head and scurried
up the narrow way half a dozen feet. A pair of rubber
handled wire snips materialized in her hand.*

*Moving fast, she approached an innocuous looking
box set into the brick of the building.*

Her little tool went snik, snik, snik.

Deputy Mark Fielder of the Commissariat of Surety
was on the carpet. His face, for once incapable of controlling inner currents, was slowly darkening.

Number One rumbled, "You were aware of the state
of the man in the street. Coaid Westley warned us

repeatedly at sessions of the Central Comita. And now, here, this massacre. Your men firing wholesale into bodies of teen-age children."

"Your Leadership! Hardly children. The affair began as a demonstration against the new draft edicts. Children are not of draft age."

Pater Riggin raised his eyebrows and murmured, "I had always thought otherwise. What is a boy of seventeen?"

They both ignored him.

"Go on," Number One said oninously. "Explain, Coaid, why over a hundred and fifty of my people were shot down on the streets of Alphacity."

There were blisters of cold sweat on the forehead of the Surety chief.

"It began fairly innocuously. My men, armed only with truncheons, attempted to break up their march. However, new elements, attracted undoubtedly as usual from curious passers-by, encouraged the youths. Some had the audacity to call out against my Surety men. The crowd swelled. My commandant in charge called for reserves."

Fielder took a handkerchief from a pocket and wiped his face.

"Nobody seems to know how the first spark was struck. Most likely it was one of the Betastani . . ."

"The what . . . !"

"The saboteurs. Was Your Leadership of the opinion that these continuing civil disturbances were spontaneous on the part of our own citizens? Please, Coaid Presidor, this much activity does not come spontaneously. It is planned. Any police agency, down through the ages, could tell you that. Riots need leaders. Most often, they need planning. Our people are too well disciplined to provide either."

Number One was dour. "Tell me more about these saboteurs before continuing with today's riot."

Deputy Fielder felt himself on stronger ground. "How long the Betastani funkers have been planning for this war is unknown but I begin to suspect that it had been even longer than our own preparations and certainly on a different level. We should have suspected the large number of exchange students that enrolled in our universities. We should . . ."

Pater Riggin murmured mildly, "At the time we thought it a wonderful opportunity to influence their minds toward our form of regime and our religion." Once again they ignored him. He didn't mind.

". . . have paid more attention to the number of their citizens who took up semi-permanent residence in Alphacity and elsewhere. At any rate, upon the declaration of war, these supposed students, tourists and temporary residents, disappeared into our streets, our mountains, our countryside. My commissariat is now of the opinion that a considerable number are highly trained ECE agents or graduates of their hush-hush *Partisan Tech*.

"What was that last?"

"A very secretive, very difficult, highly demanding institution devoted to guerrilla warfare as adapted to the modern scene. Marshal Croft-Gordon has infiltrated several of his and imprisoned. Without doubt, whoever scrambled Deputy Matheison's records was a product of *Partisan Tech*.

"At any rate, Your Leadership, evidently the Betastani espionage and guerrilla chiefs hit upon the idea of disguising large numbers of their operatives as teen-agers. Has it ever occurred to you how inconspicuous a teen-ager is upon the streets? Their very loudness of dress, their raucous voices, their condolescent gawkiness, tend to make us ignore them, usually scornfully.

"Anyway, my computers, working on what little data we can program them with, have established that there are some four thousand Betastani operatives, plus or minus three hundred and twelve, disguised as teenagers in Alphaland, at least half of them in Alphacity. Their equipment has evidently been accumulated, in various drops, over the years, some imported, some stolen."

Number One had been staring at him grimly. He rumbled now, "And why has all this not been brought to my attention sooner?"

His Surety head was suavely defensive. "Your Leadership, not even the Presidor can carry all the details of government. It was deemed basically a problem of my commissariat."

"You certainly did little to solve it. Coaid! You flat, can't you see that such situations should have been cleaned up before the Crusade began?"

"We didn't know its magnitude until the war started, Your Leadership."

His superior looked at him ominously. "You do not seem to hold down your position as well as I once thought, Coaid Fielder. It was your job to know of these spies and saboteurs." He glowered at the other for a moment. "Go on with today's riots and the ineptness of the manner in which they were handled."

"Yes, Coaid Presidor. The spark was struck, as I say, probably by a Betastani agent. My men used their riot batons. The students began to throw bricks, torn from a nearby construction job. Several Surety agents were badly wounded. Reinforcements came up, armed with stun guns. Several of these were surrounded and captured by the growing mobs. The mobs were now not young draftees alone, but older adults as well. They were shouting for the ending of the war and the resignation of your government."

"Oh, they *were!*"

"The captured stun guns were turned against my men, who, by this time, were being reinforced by armored cars and squads armed with scramblers."

Pater Riggin said in gentle accusation, "You turned

scramblers loose on an unarmed mob of our own people?"

Fielder looked at him desperately. "*Unarmed* is one way of putting it. There were thousands of them by then. They were armed with everything they could improvise. If we hadn't suppressed it all with every means we had on hand, they would have marched on the government buildings."

He wound up, saying, "As it was, it was necessary for me to call upon Marshal Croft-Gordon to send three regiments of Air Marines to help police the area."

Number One was ominous again. "This is the first I have heard of that step, Coaid. I am not sure that I like the idea of Marshal Croft-Gordon's men under arms in my capital city."

A benign looking civilian, seemingly in his late middle years, issued forth from a personal pneumatic car at one of the entry points facing Independence Square in downtown Alphacity. He looked up and down the moderately crowded street before turning to dismiss the vehicle.

As though casually, he dropped a small packet onto the seat of the car he had just left and threw the control to dismiss it.

Even as he straightened, two inconspicuously garbed men grasped him by either arm.

"All right, fella," one snarled. "What was that you left in the pneumatic, a grenade?"

"I—I beg your pardon?"

One of them flashed a Surety badge. "Come along with us, Pop. You've had it. You got any proof you're a Alphaland citizen and loyal to His Leadership, the Presidor?"

"Help! Help," their prisoner screamed suddenly, attempting to wrench away.

Five or six youngsters, dressed in the current foofaraw

87

affected by juvenile delinquents and adolescents in general, came jostling forward.

They surrounded the two Surety men and their captive, yelling, pushing close, complaining vociferously.

"Let 'im go, you two crooks!"

"Hey, stop hitting my father, you big funker!"

"They're robbin' this old man! Pickpockets!"

"Let 'em go, you yokes!"

A crowd began to gather, jostling, shoving, trying to see. It was a busy corner; the crowd grew geometrically.

Unseen, one of the youths slid his hand under his jacket to emerge with a short bladed, icepick-like weapon. He jabbed it, underhanded, into the spine of the heavy-set Surety agent before him. The man groaned softly and collapsed.

Far beneath them, in the city's pneumatic transport system, the innocent packet blew lustily, wrecking a central shuttle area.

For once the dignity of age had escaped from Academecian Philip McGivern. His face was a confusion of conflicting expressions, his hands were trembling.

Number One considered the aged economist dourly. The elderly, he decided, forgetting his own years, collapsed quickly under unwonted pressures.

He made no attempt to encourage the Old Hand companion of the days of his revolutionary seizure of power.

"Your report," he said curtly.

"Jim," the other blurted. "The whole economy's tottering. It was bad enough, the mess made of the financial system. John Matheison's been doing yeoman's work, toiling arduously day and night, to make some sort of order out of the chaos."

"But . . ." Number One led him on.

"But, Jim . . ."

"We're in formal audience, Coaid. Don't call me by personal name."

"Uh . . . Yes, Your Leadership. My pardons. Your Leadership, we've found out what happened to the Betastani fleet."

This was not news to the Presidor, but he held his peace for the moment. Undoubtedly, there were new angles.

"Your Leadership, they didn't exactly go into hiding. They submerged and dispersed, the whole navy. They've become commerce raiders. If there's any manner in which they can keep from standing and fighting, they do."

"Funkers," his superior rumbled angrily.

"No, no, it's not that." The old man was shaking his head miserably. "Jim, it's obviously long planned. I've been looking into this submarine raider business, checking way back through history. There were two major wars back on early Earth where such means of warfare almost won a conflict that otherwise couldn't have possibly succeeded. It is estimated that had Hitler been able to have kept only fifty submarines operative throughout his war, he would have brought his opponents to their knees."

"What's this got to do with here and now?"

The palsied socioeconomist took it up. "The Betastani ships are all submergible, of course. They have given up acting as a fleet and all of their craft have taken up raiding our commerce. Your Leadership, our glorious navy can't begin to defend our more than five thousand merchantmen. The Betastani act as though each of their units were expendable. They dash in to the attack no matter what the odds and would rather sink a merchant ship than a battle cruiser. In fact, several of our Coaid admirals contend that they're a mistake; they just bunch up our ships and make them more vulnerable and easier to find."

"Sum up the situation, Coaid! What does it mean in terms of the war effort?"

"Ordinarily. Your Leadership, Alphaland is all but self-sufficient. But not in time of war. The expenditure of raw materials in our munitions factories are enormous. We need copper, chrome, lead, zinc. Eventually we will need . . ."

Number One held up a hand. "All right. The situation isn't expected to last long enough for this to be an issue. The conflict will be over before it becomes disastrous. Almost all Betastan has been overrun, their armies have collapsed or are dissolving. As soon as we can locate and arrest their underground government, we can force them to sign a peace. Our recovery will be immediate. We'll seize their treasury to buttress our own. And the neutral nations, seeing our strength of position, will rally to our support."

Pater Riggin said mildly, "The neutral nations, Jim? I understand that Gambania, Morrisland and New Zambia severed relations with us this morning, and that their mobilization is almost complete."

McGivern was saying in agony, in refutation of his leader's words, "Originally, the computers said the war would last less than two and a half months. Later they said less than a month. But now the war's going into its fifth month, and we're in a worse situation than when it began. We can't keep this up, Jim, we can't keep it up!"

"Don't call me Jim, you damned funker!" Number One roared.

The Old Hand stared at him, shocked.

The skipper of the M.S. Freedomland came up behind his third officer and the two deckmen who were leaning over the starboard rail. He rapped, "What in the name of the Holy damned Ultimate are you doing?"

They turned, grinning.

"Look, those kids down there."

The captain looked over the side. Below were four or five kids on a makeshift raft and two others working out of a battered rowboat; all of them were attired in raggedy bathing trunks and were yelling and shouting up to the crew members.

"What'n the hell do they want?" the captain growled. "We're almost loaded. You men get to your damned posts."

The third said, "They're diving for centavos, Skipper. The local coinage. Here, watch." He tossed two or three coins into the water.

Immediately, it was a matter of bottoms up, and the kids dove into the darkish waters.

"They gettum, every one," one of the crewmen said, laughing. "You'd think that water was too dirty."

"I'll be damned," the skipper said. "Like nardy dolphins, aren't they?" He stuck his hand into a trouser pocket to check his change.

Down below, one of the dolphins had pulled up against the ship's hull. A small plastic packet was in his hands. He placed it carefully about ten feet abaft the bow and about two feet above the keel. It stuck magnetically. If information was correct, and it was, the fuel tanks of the M.S. Freedomland commenced at this point.

The swimmer, his lungs beginning to ache, threw a small stud on the side of the plastic container and headed back for the surface; in his hand was a coin which he had extracted from his belt, rather than finding it on the harbor bottom.

Behind him, the little packet was going tic-toc.

IX

TEMPLE BISHOP STOCKWATER, trailed by two Temple Vicars, proceeded benignly along the corridors of the Commissariat of Information.

Passersby widened their eyes, came to a quick halt and touched fingers to lips in religious salute. He nodded piously and murmured blessings as he progressed.

In the central offices of the deputy, he made his way, in the slow shuffle of the religious, to the desk of Senior Secretary Jet Pirincin, who was all but popeyed at his presence. She began to come quickly erect, her fingers immediately to lips.

But he held out a soft, white hand in placation.

"Easily, daughter," he murmured. "I shall not interrupt your blessed efforts, participating in the holy Crusade. Now, that is the Coaid Deputy's office, I assume?"

"Yes . . . yes . . . Your Blessedness. I . . . I . . ."

"Don't bother yourself, daughter." He blessed her and moved on.

Upon the entry of the United Temple's representative to the Central Comita into his inner sanctum, Ross Westley hurried to his feet. The visit was unprecedented. Although Temple Bishop Stockwater and he had met often in the presence of Number One, they had never before held private conversation.

The Temple Bishop smiled unctuously at him, murmured something that ended in, ". . . my son," then turned to his Temple Vicars.

It occured to Ross Westley that the two younger men were on the tall and brawny side and not overly saintly in countenance.

The Temple Bishop bade them remain outside and waited until the door was closed. He then turned his rounded face to his host.

Ross Westley indicated his most comfortable chair. "Your Blessedness, this is a great honor. Could I offer you refreshment?"

The other lowered his bulk and gave an un-bishop-like squirm to achieve complete ease. He beamed at Ross. "I have heard that the Presidor imports a beverage from Mother Earth that is quite unique. Ah, sherry, I

92

believe it is called. You wouldn't have a small amount I might sample?"

Ross was slightly taken aback. "Sherry? I believe I've read about it. But, I understand it's alcoholic, Your Blessedness."

The Temple Bishop looked at him. Finally he said, "Indeed. Then, of course, the Presidor would never touch lip to such an abomination."

Ross shrugged that part of it off. He indicated his orderbox. "I could have Coaid Pirincin bring you a sherbet."

"Never mind," the Temple Bishop said, his voice slightly less benign. "I shall, Coaid Deputy Westley, come immediately to the point."

However, he didn't; for a time, he skirted it.

He said, eyeing the other pensively, "You have, I understand, some learning in history, Coaid Wesley."

Ross, wondering still at the other's presence, said, "I had expected to become a teacher of the subject, before my father's assassination brought me to this position."

Temple Bishop Stockwater put the tips of his fingers together and beamed. "Of course. Then the following facts will not be strange to you. My son, I bid you recall the history of Western religion in the Mother Earth nation of Mexico. Most briefly, representatives of the prevailing European religion landed with the conquistadors under Cortes. They backed with their every effort the Spanish cause and were instrumental in completely destroying the religious and other institutions of the aborigines."

Ross, frowning, nodded. "Of course."

The Temple Bishop went on. "For several centuries, during the Spanish domination, this religious organization supported the Spanish in their disastrous rule of the predominantly Amerind population. When there was rebellion, they strongly sided with authority. At long last, when Europe was embroiled in the Napoleonic

Wars, Latin America revolted, including Mexico. The church lined up, as usual, with the ruling power."

Ross, still frowning, still nodded.

"However, the people won and Spain was ousted. The new government continued its attempts at reform of the institutions that had been established under the Spanish rule. But the more conservative groups, largely remnants of the older regime, fought back to the extent possible and finally invited in the so-called Emperor Maximilian, an Austrian Hapsburg, who was backed militarily by Napoleon the Third of France. The religious body supported the France-Maximilian alliance and repudiated the democratic government headed by Juárez.

"But—shall we say, unfortunately?—it was Juárez who prevailed and Maximilian was shot. Juárez, however did not long survive him and soon the government came under the dictatorship of Porfiro Días, the representative of the great landholders and most conservative elements. When the people again rose in revolt against the dictatorship, under Madero, the religious organization supported the authorities. Although Madero was killed, however, his followers eventually won and came to power."

The Bishop at last went silent and looked at Ross Westley thoughtfully. "My son, are you beginning to see my point?"

Ross shrugged. "The historian, Gibbon, pointed out in his *Decline and Fall of the Roman Empire* that established religions always support the established authority."

The United Temple representative nodded, as though the other had made some profound statement. "As it should be," he said. "However, let me finish with the example of Mexico. Four times in succession this religious group had backed the, ah, established authority, or, at least, the minority conservative elements in society. The people, at long last, had grown tired of this. So strong measures were taken against our colleagues of

94

yesteryear. Under the conservative regimes they had grown wealthy indeed, controlling a great deal of the property of the country. But the new government now confiscated this property. They passed laws against alliances between the State and Church. They prevented religious orders from teaching in the schools. They went so far as to forbid priests and nuns from appearing in the streets in religious garb. They passed laws preventing them from soliciting alms in public. They even passed a law preventing church bells from ringing more than one minute in duration at a time." The Bishop registered indignation. "It was a horrible persecution."

Ross said, "Your Blessedness, I am afraid I am dense. I don't see what you're driving at."

Temple Bishop Stockwater nodded. "My son, the United Temple must take a lesson from this example and other similar ones. Although it has a duty to established authority, it has a greater duty still to itself and its mission to bring all to the eventual glory of the Holy Ultimate. No longer can a religious organization in all consciousness stand on the sidelines when an unpopular authority is running athwart the desires of the people."

Ross Westley couldn't believe he was translating this double-talk correctly. He stared at the other.

The Temple Bishop looked into his eyes. "My son, there are others who are of similar belief. I pray you are with us."

"With you! What are you suggesting?"

The other smiled benignly. "There will be a meeting of our farseeing, idealistic group almost immediately, my son. Will you come with me?"

Ross Westley was still staring. He was trying desperately to assimilate this. If it meant what he thought it meant . . . He came suddenly to his feet.

"Let's go," he said.

At the door, he stood aside to let the older man precede him. The two goon-like Temple Vicars fell in

95

behind. For a brief moment a suspicion hit him. What would have happened had he refused to accompany the United Temple representative?

The group passed Jet Pirincin who followed them with her eyes, a surprise in their depths, until they had passed completely from the offices.

She thought about it for a moment, reached down slowly and picked up a handphone, unequipped with screen. She said into it, "Relay this to T."

Outside the Commissariat of Information building was the elaborate, almost flamboyant, hover-limousine of a Temple Bishop, the insignia of the United Temple prominent on its side. Behind was parked a small vehicle, more decorous but with the emblem on both doors and rear. For the Temple Vicars cum guards, Ross told himself.

He was accorded the honor of riding with the Temple Bishop, wondering, as they drove, at the destination.

He might have known. Temple Bishop Stockwater dialed the coordinates of the War Ministry and they were there within the quarter hour, their clearing control dividing the city traffic for them. They wouldn't have taken any longer in the pneumatic.

They spoke only once during the ride, Ross Westley spending the time in hurried attempt to think this all out.

He had said, "Who else will be there?"

"That remains to be seen, my son," the other had said smoothly.

The car took them to a back entrance, through highly guarded byways, and the major of the Surety men posted there did no more than take in the car's insignia before coming to the salute.

They stepped out of the luxurious vehicle and Ross stood to one side to let the berobed older man precede him. He followed in silence. The Temple Vicars remained outside, still seated in their car.

At the entry, they passed two more guards, one of whom was seated at a control board. A light flickered red.

The other Surety agent stepped before them respectfully, but with his right hand only inches from his holstered sidearm.

"Coaid," he said to Ross, "you're carrying a shooter."

Ross looked at him. "I'm a full Deputy and the country's at war. Why shouldn't I carry a shooter?"

"Sorry, Coaid Deputy. You'll have to leave it here."

Ross looked at the Temple Bishop who nodded with the same benign expression.

He shrugged, brought the gun from his shoulder holster and tendered it to the guard, then followed after the older man.

There were four more guards before a heavy door. Two of them flung it open, somewhat dramatically, Ross thought, upon Temple Bishop Stockwater's approach.

Inside, around a conference table, were those whom, after all, Ross Westley had actually expected to see. Well, there were several others as well. In fact, he was somewhat surprised to find his own Assistant Deputy, Job Bauserman.

There were a full dozen of the Central Comita and a check revealed all the more important faces, save, possibly, that of Philip McGivern of Socioeconomics. *One of the Old Hands*, Ross told himself. He had probably not even been approached.

Mark Fielder, the Surety head, broke off the whispered conversation he was having at one end of the room with Marshal Croft-Gordon, and said, smiling his cold smile, "I assume this is all, Coaids. Shall we call the conference to order?"

He strode to the head of the table and took up the

gavel there, saving them, however, from the necessity of hearing it bang.

Ross Westley secured a chair at one end, two seats away from anyone else. He watched and listened warily.

Mark Fielder had evidently appointed himself spokesman as well as chairman. As soon as they had all found places, he looked out over them suavely, then began.

"Coaids, it hardly needs to be pointed out that Alphaland is in a crisis. Due to the most inept handling of a relatively simple situation, we now face disaster unless strong steps are taken by those of us assembled here. Frankly, and as is well known to you all, our leader has failed to rise to the occasion."

"Right!" somebody growled.

"If we are to rescue the situation, we must act with dispatch."

Marshal Croft-Gordon was on his feet, his swagger stick banging on his leg. "Then let's stop talking and start acting! I'll tell you all this: I'll take no more orders from the arrogant flat!"

Fielder held up a hand, though smiling his understanding. "Please, Marshal. Some preliminary decisions must be made."

Jon Matheison, of Finance, called out, "One immediate problem. Who is to step into his shoes? Who among us is strong enough to take over the office of Presidor?"

"Who's Number One, in short?" one of the assistant deputies present called.

Fielder was shaking his head. He looked at Ross Westley and said, "I'm sure our deputy of propaganda would agree with me in this. It is not going to be enough to remove the present Presidor and place another in his office. The people are going to want the outer semblance, at least, of a complete change. That we can sell. Am I right, Coaid Westley?"

Ross shifted in his chair, all eyes upon him. "If you

can sell them a change at all, it had better be something revolutionary, all right. Half measures would be probably worse than none at all."

"Correct!" the Surety head applauded.

Temple Bishop Stockwater said worriedly, "Now, my children, let us not become too radical here. We would not wish to disturb established institutions."

Job Bauserman, unduly articulate in this gathering of his superiors, Ross thought with some surprise, said, "But we'll have to seem to disturb them, Coaids. The candidate for office, whether he means to attain it through force or by ballot, promises great reform in the attaining. Living up to it, later, is another matter."

Fielder looked at the propaganda man thoughtfully. "You are quite correct, of course, Coaid. We must promise them the moon, as the ancient expression goes."

Matheison added, "And later deliver green cheese."

Fielder took direction again. "So simply changing the Presidor would be insufficient. I propose, Coaids, that a triumvirate be nominated here, this afternoon. And that elections be promised within a year after our coming to power."

"Elections!" the Marshal blurted, unbelievingly. "You mean *real* elections?"

The Temple Bishop, too, led the objections. "My son, much though I am in sympathy with democratic institutions, and look forward to the day when they are practical, surely it is realized by all present that our good people are not, at present, capable of voting intelligently. They lack, ah, the educational background, the, ah, intelligence. Until they are arrived at a higher level than now prevails, it falls upon us of the, ah, better classes to lead them."

Ross Westley looked at the holy man. It was a cry heard down through the ages. He wondered if Stockwater had ever read of the fact that most primitive men, long before the advent of writing, not to speak of education, ruled themselves democratically. Not that Ross had any intention of bringing forth the subject in this gathering.

Fielder held up a hand again, the hands holding the gavel, and chuckled without humor. "Coaids, please. You evidently failed to hear me. I said that we would *promise* elections. Once in power, various emergencies can arise—a threat of the Karlists attempting to put their own candidates on the ballot, or some such. We can face such problems when they confront us; certainly no one here is so foolish as to suggest mob rule."

"Amen," the Temple Bishop murmured.

Fielder pressed on. "A ruling triumvirate, fraternally united, will be a departure from one man control, such as the Presidor has exercised. It will seem, and on the surface be, a radical change and appear to herald still more definite reform. However, in actuality, such a triumvirate will continue to reflect the desires of this, our body, the Central Comita."

Bauserman said, "I suggest that the name of the Comita be changed, as well as the title of every official in it, save, of course, the representative of the United Temple." Here he nodded his head to the Temple Bishop. "The Temple, of course, remains unchanging, as it should be, down through the ages. But the Commissariat of Finance should have its name changed to something like the Ministry of the Treasury. The Commissariat of Information could become the Department of Public Knowledge."

Fielder was nodding encouragingly. "Coaid Bauserman is obviously going to be a valuable member of the new regime. We must make as many surface changes as possible."

Somebody called, "All right, but who's to be on this triumvirate?"

Fielder looked at the speaker. "Among ourselves, of course, we are Coaids and equals. The actual trio will be meaningless. I suggest we now nominate our three figure-heads, our supposed chiefs of state."

Ross grunted inwardly. Figureheads, his aching back. He already knew who was to succeed Number One, given a success of this putsch. And he strongly suspected that it had been worked out long ago.

Matheison called, "I nominate Marshal Croft-Gordon, our most noted hero. Next to the present Presidor, certainly the best known public figure in Alphaland."

"Second," someone called. Ross noted idly that the seconder was in uniform.

"Our chairman, Coaid Fielder," someone else called.

The holder of the gavel held up a hand. "Now, consider well, Coaids. Remember, in actuality, our three whil be but figureheads for this Comita. However, is it wise that a police official be on the group?"

"Absolutely," Bauserman called. "The military and police must be seen to be represented. The iron fist within the silken glove."

"Second the motion," Franklin Wilkonson, the geo-politician, called out.

One of the Old Hands, Ross told himself bitterly. Shoulder to shoulder with Number One on the barricades.

"Jon Matheison," someone else called out and was seconded.

Ross nodded to himself. He had called it. Croft-Gordon, Fielder and Matheison. The other two didn't know it, but eventually that triumvirate was going to slim down to one man again. He might not call himself the Presidor, but eventually, Ross had no doubt, Mark Fielder would stand alone at the head of government. Neither of the other two had the capability to hold ultimate power.

He listened, but largely unhearing as they droned through other proposals.

Finally, Fielder brought it to the crux. "We are, then,

in complete agreement. Number One has failed us. It is our duty to take over the reins of government."

"Who's going to bell the cat?" Ross said, evenly.

All eyes came to him, most faces frowning.

Ross said, "Who's going to take on the job of getting through Number One's Surety and informing him he has just been demoted from the job he's held for almost half a century?"

Fielder pursed his lips. "That has been worked out, Coaid. Marshal Croft-Gordon, Deputy Matheison and I will request audience with the Presidor. We will inform him of the changes."

"And what will his guard have to say about that?"

Fielder arched his eyebrows. "My dear Coaid Westley, it is I who appoints the Surety guards to protect the Presidor."

Ross nodded. He should have known the answer. Evidently, Number One was not to survive the audience with his three top deputies.

Fielder repeated himself. "We are, then, in complete agreement?"

Ross, who had been slouched in his chair, trying to keep from contemplating the result of what he knew he was going to do, came deliberately to his feet. He looked around at the rest of them, one by one. Deep within himself he was amazed. All this was not in his basically retiring nature.

"I guess this is the vote," he said. "This is where we take our stand."

He looked at Wilkonson. "I understand that you, Co-aid, along with my father and Number One, were one of the original revolutionary committee. One of the hand-ful who revolted against the takeover of the Karlists. Who else is left of that group? Only Academecian McGivern, I suppose, the party theoretician. I notice Coaid Mc-Givern isn't here."

102

Fielder said coldly, "He met with an unfortunate accident, shortly after being approached, Coaid."

Ross nodded. He looked at Marshal Croft-Gordon, who appeared to be building up a head of steam. "And the good Marshal, although not an Old Hand, also fought in the war, if party history serves me. At first as a sergeant, but under the wing of Number One he rose quickly in rank until at last he is supreme head of the military."

Ross turned his gaze on Mark Fielder. "And our Deputy of Surety. As I recall, a nephew of one of the now deceased Old Hands who recommended him highly to Number One. And he, as a favor, saw our present chairman, and triumvir to be, promoted and promoted again."

Fielder said ominously, "What are you getting to, Coaid?"

Ross shrugged. "Isn't it obvious, Coaids? I am the son of Franklin Westley, another of the Old Hands. Frankly, I am a misfit in my position. However, I am not a traitor, although I find myself increasingly against our present government. My single vote is against this coup d'état. I suggest instead that the full Central Comita be convened and that the Presidor be allowed to defend himself before it. If he cannot do so, I suggest that an immediate election be held and a new government be chosen by all elements of the population."

An angry buzz had already started through the room.

But Fielder held up a hand.

He said, his mouth twisted in half mockery, "You will notice, Coaids, that the Commissariat of Information is represented by Assistant Deputy Bauserman, as well as by the estimable Ross Westley, who by his own confession is a misfit in his position. Coaid Bauserman was invited to this meeting in anticipation of just such an occurrence as this. Indeed, it was he who first brought to my attention, as Deputy of Surety, the fact that Coaid Westley is not quite as veracious as he might project when he tells us so nobly that he cannot act the traitor."

"What are you driving at?" Ross growled.

"It was through Coaid Bauserman that my men first became aware of the fact that Coaid Westley had fallen under the feminine charms of a Betastani national now known to be a leader of saboteurs, ECE agents and guerrillas taking active action against our forces here in Alphacity and elsewhere. Further, our own ECE agents in New Betatown inform us that the Betastani General Staff is in possession of information that could only have originated in meetings of the Central Comita."

Fielder's eyes flashed out over the conference table. "This man is a traitor to Alphaland, Coaids!"

He turned dramatically and pointed to the door. "You will leave at once." His voice went into a sneer. "*Coaid* Westley."

Ross took a deep breath, opened his mouth as though to retort, closed it again and shrugged. Without further word, he turned and marched toward the door.

Angry voices echoed after him. He ignored them.

He opened the heavy door and stepped out into the Corridor beyond. Two Surety agents fell in step beside him.

"This way," one of them grunted.

They departed the Ministry of War by another route than the one by which he had entered.

He wondered emptily about the scene just through, still amazed at his own temerity. Had he supported Fielder and his gang, would the other have kept the secret of Tilly Trice and his connection with her? He didn't know. Perhaps he could have found a position in the new government for himself, had he kowtowed to the other. It made no difference now. Nor did much else.

He had to smile inwardly in self-deprecation. It was only a matter or time, anyway, before Job Bauserman got his job. The Holy Ultimate knew, the man was more capable of holding it.

His two guards ushered him downstairs to a dark garage and to a Surety police semi-armored car. He was hustled into the back seat, a bully-boy on each side, and noted in mild surprise that the vehicle was chauffeur driven rather than being auto. It must have been designed to be used in rough country where coordinates couldn't be dialed.

They took off, zooming up a ramp to the boulevard outside.

"Where are we going?" Ross said, not expecting an answer.

He didn't get it.

The eternal goons, he thought.

They turned a corner, and immediately the driver smashed on the brakes. Careening toward them was a fast moving civilian car, another immediately behind it, as though the two were racing.

Racing? Here in the downtown area of Alphacity? Both cars seemed overflowing with kids.

The Surety driver swerved frantically, and uselessly. The lead racing car sideswiped them one way. He spun the wheel in desperation. The following car swiped them on the opposite side. There was screaming and rasping of tortured metal.

And over they went, rolling, crashing ultimately against a store front.

And all went black for Ross Westley.

Far, far away, and as though in a dream, he seemed to see Tilly, done up as she had been dressed that day when she'd told him she belonged to an archery club—in boy's clothing, a Robin Hood-like cap on her head. She was bending, now, over one of the Surety men who had been thrown out onto the pavement. She was looking over the papers she had evidently pulled from his pockets, seemingly in no great hurry. She held a small shooter in one hand, as though she were very used to having a shooter in hand.

And then the black rolled in again.

X

HE CAME OUT of it to feel his head cushioned warmly and to feel the sensation of rapid movement still. Confusedly, he thought it must be impossible. The vehicle in which he rode had turned over.

A faraway voice said, "He isn't hurt badly."

Another voice—was there a feminine quality?—said ominously, "He'd better not be. You cloddies are on the precipitous side when it comes to rescues."

Still a third voice said, in defense, "That Surety car was armored, Till. How'd you expect us to take it, especially with such short warning?"

Ross opened his eyes. "What in Zen's happened?" he asked.

Tilly Trice grinned down at him. "The cavalry arrived in the nick of time," she said. She patted his head. "Now you relax. We'll have a medico look at you shortly."

His head was in her lap. He closed his eyes again. Who was he to argue?

He tried to make sense of his position.

Evidently, the underground guerrillas were even more highly organized than the Alphaland authorities had suspected. Somehow, they had known of that meeting. Somehow they had suspected his arrest would follow. Somehow they had rescued him, for whatever purpose. It was quite a collection of somehows.

He must have dozed off again. When next he brought his mind to bear on his surroundings, he was being hustled, albeit gently, from the car in which he had been riding into what looked like an ordinary commercial garage, though of considerable size.

Their vehicle had pulled to the far end where customers could hardly have seen it. He was helped out, supported at each arm, and half led, half carried, into a room beyond. It appeared to be an office of some sort. Someone pushed a large file which swung on hinges, revealing still another room beyond.

It brought back to memory the cement bunker under Tilly's bookstore. And he vaguely wondered just how long the Bestastani *had* been preparing for this offbeat war.

They put him into a lower bunk and he shortly felt the administrations of someone who was obviously a medico.

A voice said from great distances, "A mild concussion. There is nothing seriously wrong."

Ross Westley felt protest. Nothing wrong, indeed. Everything was wrong.

Number One, Presidor of the Free Democratic Commonwealth of Alphaland, glared at his three top associates.

"For thirty years," he said heavily, "it has been a basic of this government that I not be disturbed upon retiring to my private apartments. Even the Presidor needs rest eventually."

Mark Fielder shook his head, as though in regret. "Your Leadership, the most fast rule must on occasion have its exception."

Marshal Croft-Gordon, already dark of face, simply returned his superior's glare.

Jon Matheison was not a man of action. His eyes darted uncomfortably about the room, taking in the bar, the fireplace, and the rounded Pater Riggin seated seated quietly beside it.

Fielder said to Number One's old companion, "Pater, I suggest you leave. This conference is of first priority."

Pater Riggin's eyes went to his lifelong companion. "Jim?"

Number One, eyes narrow now, said, "Remain where you are, Rig. It occurs to me that I may wish to have witnesses to this indignity, later."

Fielder shrugged, "As you will. It is on your own head, Pater. In the future, you may be sorry to have been a witness."

"I rather doubt it," the Temple Monk said mildly. "I am an old man, my son. There are few threats that could frighten me."

Marshal of the Armies Rupert Croft-Gordon rasped, "Let's get to the point!"

"Yes," Number One said, looking at his Surety Deputy. "Let us get to the point. The first point is that all three of you are dismissed from your offices."

Jon Matheison giggled nervously.

Mark Fielder let his head go left and right slowly. "That is why we have come. The opposite is true. It is you who have failed in your duties and have been dismissed by the Central Comita."

The nostrils of the supreme chief of the Alphaland government flared. "The Comita has no power to remove me, as you well know, Fielder. However, we shall immediately convene that body." His eyes went briefly to the Temple Monk. "Rig, do me the kindness to summon my guard."

Fielder looked at the seated old man. "Don't bother, Pater. The former Presidor has no guards. In fact, he hasn't had any for over a month."

"Are you drivel happy?" Number One roared.

"They are *my* guards," Mark Fielder said mockingly.

Alphaland's strong man stomped to his private bar, took up a bottle with shaking hand and poured a heavy slug into a tumbler. He took up the glass and spun back to them.

"You fools! You can't attempt this in time of war. The people will tear you apart. Besides all that, it will most likely mean a collapse of the war effort. Civil war at the very least."

Jon Matheison had at last found courage to speak. He shrilled, "It is you who would be torn apart. The war's impossibly unpopular. The peace riots are everywhere. We will take power on a platform of ending the war quickly. The Commissariat of Propaganda is ready to release a broadcast from the triumvirate that it will immediately go to Betastan and terminate the war as soon as possible."

Number One threw the drink back over his palate.

"Traitors!" he rumbled. "Surrounded by traitors, supposedly my friends."

Pater Riggin said mildly, "You should have read your Machiavelli better, Jim. Ultimately, a prince must have no intimate friends."

Marshal Croft-Gordon said, "Enough of this nardy blather. What are we arguing about? It's all over. Call the guards in. Convene the court martial." He grimaced his hatred, repressed for so many years. "The sooner he's liquidated, the better. Anyone flat enough to think in terms of supporting him will be left leaderless."

Number One poured another drink and chuckled bitter laughter. "Sergeant Croft-Gordon of the paratroopers. No, you weren't so aristocratic in those days, were you, Rupert? It was Rupert Gordon then. The hyphenated Croft, your mother's name, was added after I had promoted you over more capable officers because I was cloddy enough to think you capable of gratitude."

Pater Riggin looked at him wanly and murmured beneath his breath, "Dreamer."

Mark Fielder said, "Enough. Let's go." He made a

sour mouth. "You first, *Your Leadership.*" He brought a small handgun from his tunic pocket.

Both the Marshal and John Matheison did the same.

The Marshal motioned with his toward the door.

Number One, still enraged beyond the point of being conscious of physical danger, stood stiff, as though refusing to budge.

Up until this point, Pater Riggin had sat quietly by the fire, the customary ancient book in his lap, one finger holding his place. When he sighed and set it aside, not an eye followed his movement. He did not have the color to draw interest in this heated conflict between strong men.

He slipped a pale hand into a pocket of his robe and flicked, rather than threw, a small pellet between the triumvirate and his lifelong companion.

It burst into a very fireworks of smoke, bright flame and—they were soon to find—nausea gas.

He came erect, surprisingly nimble for such a sedentary type. There was a handkerchief at his nostrils. He bustled forward, grasping the deposed dictator by the arm.

"Quickly now, Jim. This way."

A beam from Fielder's gun burned a ray across the room, striking nothing but a tapestry on a far wall.

The Marshal was shouting incoherently.

Mark Fielder spun around and was pounding upon the door he had entered through ten minutes before. "Guards! Guards!"

Jon Matheison had slipped to the floor and was holding his throat and sobbing in terror.

The Temple Monk's grasp was surprisingly firm. "This way. Jim. Holy Ultimate, move!"

Number One's eyes were streaming and already his stomach and lungs seemed to churn. He stumbled along, his mind reeling at the developments of the quarter hour.

He was led through a room, back through a passage. He knew his own quarters, of course, but the confusion was upon him to the point that he really did not know which way he went.

Suddenly the air was clear and he was in an alleyway. Vaguely he recognized it, though circumstance had not taken him this way for so many years he could not remember. It was sort of servant entrance.

Pater Riggin, a slight tremor in his voice, said ruefully, "We may now pray to the Holy Ultimate that our good Deputy of Surety did not go to the bother of completely surrounding the Presidor's palace. Remain here for a moment, Jim. Please don't stray. I am an old man and cannot handle too many variables. Besides"—there was a wry humor—"I am not too practiced in rescuing deposed chiefs of state."

He was gone.

Number One, the gas relieving him of all dignity, leaned against the stone of the alleyway and vomited desperately. His eyes burned so that he could hardly see, his stomach churned.

The voice of Pater Riggin was back.

"Here. In here, Jim. Quickly. They'll burn their way through those doors in moments."

The former dictator was hustled into a small two-seater hover-car. He did not know why, nor where they were bound. And he cared less.

Ross Westley had come awake possibly an hour earlier, but had not brought attention to himself. There were half a dozen others in the long barracks-like room, but none that he recognized. Three or four of them were bandaged—obviously wounded; he suspected the others there were too. They were remaining in their bunks, similar to his own situation.

He considered his position. Certainly, his need was escape.

111

But how, and to where? He could think of no place to go. Once again, he had been a long-term fool. He was enough of the historian to know that in the past, high ranking officials of totalitarian regimes made a practice of establishing funds in a secure foreign land, or more than one. Given collapse of government or personal misadventure, one could then live out one's life in luxurious retirement.

But not he! What a flat! What a common yoke, not to have feathered his nest when resources were unlimited.

But this wasn't the time for self-recrimination. He had to act. Now. Immediately. He was in the hands of the enemy.

But at that he had to smile his self-deprecation. Who wasn't the enemy? He had no friends.

It occurred to him that it had been a long time since Ross Westley had had friends. What top government deputy of a totalitarian regime has friends? Drinking companions, had he wanted them, in large number, in spite of the anti-alcohol stricture of the United Temple, yes. Blondes, brunettes, redheads, or any combination of the three, yes. Mopsies galore to anticipate his any variation of vice, were he so inclined, yes. Those to fawn, those to agree with his silliest statement, those to encourage him on to any secret desire, yes. But a friend?

He thought of Tilly Trice.

Yes, Till. She had milked him of information when he was infatuated with her, and now, at the end of the road, had given the final humiliation of kidnapping him.

And at that point, Tilly herself entered the bunker, immediately followed by Centurion Combs and a dozen others of the youthful appearing guerrillas that were her command.

Combs, his face whitish, had his right arm in a sling. Two of the others seemed to bear minor wounds. Tilly herself was filthy dirty, as though she had rolled on the ground. She had lost her Robin Hood cap and her hair, short-cut, was a mess.

She did manage, however, to come up with a characteristically pert grin when she saw he was awake.

"Hi, lover-mine," she said, coming over. "Those Surety men of yours are beginning to look a little more stute. They're catching on to even the better of our little fun and games bits. They're evidently now in the silly position of arresting all boy scouts and such uniformed teen-age groups."

He shook his head. "It's just a matter of time, Till. They'll get you."

She twisted her small mouth. "Perhaps. But there are others. Besides, it's not just us, anymore. Your own people are beginning to take to the field. This country is becoming one fouled up confusion, Rossie."

She sat down on a stool next to his bed. "How are you feeling?"

He said in a burst of candor, "I'm fine. I've just been figuring out a plan of escape."

"Escape," Combs said curtly, over a cup of coffee he'd just drawn for himself one handed, from a huge urn on a mess table. "Did you labor under the illusion we'd stop you?"

"That'll be all, Centurion," Tilly Trice said.

Ross scowled at her. "You mean I'm free to go?"

"Why not? Have you someplace better to be?"

Then it came back to him—the circumstances under which he had been seized by the Betastani irregulars. He flushed.

"I suppose I should be thanking you."

"Oh, don't bother." One of the other seeming-youngsters grinned. "It was no trouble at all, getting you away from those Surety goons."

"Shut up, Altshuler," Tilly said. She looked back to Ross. "What're your plans, Rossie?"

"I have none," he said bitterly. "Fielder, Croft-Gordon and the rest are overthrowing Number One. I don't know why I didn't string along. I suppose it was because of my old man. He wasn't really very smart about politics, but he was, well, loyal. He thought Number One was the only answer to combat the Karlists. I couldn't betray his memory, I suppose."

Combs looked at him and then at Tilly, his expression surly. At what, Ross didn't know. Combs didn't seem to think much of Ross Westley.

Tilly turned to another of the guerrillas who stood to one side, ultra-weary, a cup of coffee in one hand. He had been watching, unspeaking.

She said, "Manuel, you'd better get that on the air. Either Number One is overthrown, or, if not, our broadcasting it will precipitate the crisis. In fact, it'd help if Alphaland first heard of his mutinied deputies from a Betastan source."

Manuel Gonzales put the coffee down and said, "It's doubtful if there's a station left in Betastan capable of planet-wide broadcasting. The Alphaland troops have overrun them all." But he moved toward a corner of electronic equipment at the far end of the bunker.

Tilly said, "We don't need a station of our own. Just so we can beam the information to a neutral—if there are any neutrals left."

"What is that supposed to mean?" Ross scowled up at her. He began to feel foolish, remaining in his bunk after admitting that nothing was wrong with him. Especially since the others seemed so completely exhausted, Tilly included. He swung his legs over the side of the bed and sat erect, preparatory to coming to his feet.

"About the neutrals? They're lining up, Rossie." Her mouth twisted wry humor. "And I'm afraid that, in choosing sides, yours hasn't come up with many pals."

She had slumped down on a bench at the mess

table nearest him, and he changed his mind about standing.

He shook his head at her. "I don't see how you've done what you have. Admittedly, you've shot your bolt by now; your government is in hiding, your army has deteriorated into small units, except in a few places like the Tatra Mountains. Your navy is scattered or sunk and your air fleet either shot down or in hiding at minor fields. But what amazes me is that you were able to hold out as long as you have. The computers . . ."

Combs chuckled sourly, as he drew some more coffee. "You've been listening to your own propaganda, fella. We're still going strong. It's you Alphaland yokes who're disintegrating. Sure, our army has split up into small units. That was the plan. Sure, maybe half our navy has been sunk. It's expendable. But where's your merchant fleet, eh? It's not doing so well. And what's the effect on your economy? Fella, this war is just getting under way."

Ross looked at Tilly rather than at the speaker, and he was frowning.

Tilly said, reasonably, "Rossie, never underestimate the enemy. Never expect him to do what you want him to do."

"I don't know what you're talking about."

"Your Marshal Croft-Gordon and his general staff, with all their computers. Figuring out exactly what we would do, were we logical and consistent. Figuring out just where we would logically make our stand. How we would defend our cities against your bombers and missiles. How our fleet would sail forth to do what it could against your stronger, more numerous vessels. Don't you see the only answer, Rossie?"

He continued to scowl his lack of understanding.

"Rossie, we simply couldn't be logical and consistent. Your computers were exactly right. They were quite infallible . . ."

"Ha!" he snorted.

". . . if we had been logical and consistent, or, worse still, if we had resorted to our own few computers to give us our answers to military problems."

She shook her head. "Rossie, what is the best defense against a mechanized army, complete with every latest device of the military, including computer-brains and data banks containing every bit of military information accumulated on any of the United Planets?"

He looked at her blankly.

She continued. "What is the defense against a man in an ultra-tank, with enough firepower at his control to equal a division of the time of the historic World Wars of old Mother Earth? What is such a soldier's potential enemy?"

He was still blank.

She told him. "A man with a pair of pliers and perhaps a knife, a shotgun. Of course, a small amount of dynamite or even more efficient explosive helps also."

She could see he was still foundering after her.

"Rossie, have you ever heard of the Yugoslavian, Tito?"

"Vaguely."

"Very well. Along about the middle of the Second War, when the Nazi star was at its ascendency, the Germans decided that Yugoslavia was needed in their camp. In a matter of days, they had sent an ultimatum, bombed Belgrade, the capital, into ruins, dispatched their panzers down the roads of the little country, capturing every town that counted. The king fled, the army capitulated. The whole world realized that little Yugoslavia had been defeated, as so many of the smaller European nations had been defeated by the Nazi hosts."

She looked at him mockingly. "Everybody realized the defeat but the Yugoslavians. They took to the mountains. Small groups at first, slowly to be united. They fought, initially as individuals or in small squads. Slowly they grew to company, brigade, regiment and then division size. Large areas were under their domination, though the cities and roads remained in German hands. By the time of Stalingrad, the Germans had two full Army Corps tied up in Yugoslavia fighting Tito and his partisans. You're a historian. Do you remember the significance of Stalingrad, Rossie? It was the turning point of the war. Adolph the Aryan could have used those two army corps at the time of crisis."

He nodded, slowly. "So you decided to follow the example of Tito."

"Oh, more than that. We improved considerably. You see, in the past, Rossie, guerrillas were found in their own country after it had been overrun by the enemy. But we extrapolated in the field of partisan warfare and decided to carry it into the aggressor land. In the past, saboteurs were single individuals who stealthily crept about planting an occasional bomb here, blowing up a bridge there, gimmicking up some valuable machinery the other place. We decided on parlaying that up to a grander scale. When we could see the chips were all soon to be down, we planted thousands of saboteurs-to-be here in your—" she made her typical pouting face— "Free Democratic Commonwealth.

"But that obviously wasn't going to be enough. We also acted illogically in not utilizing our fleet to protect our coasts against your own ships. We let our coastal cities capitulate, undefended, and our ships struck at your Achilles heel, your economy. Nor did our army stand bravely and attempt to defend our frontiers, as your computers expected. Instead, they cut for the rear, giving up space in return for finding a better field of battle. Or, indeed, splitting up and becoming guerrillas on our own soil."

Tilly came to an end with a pert snort. "Combs is right, Rossie. We haven't *begun* to lose this war, at this point."

Ross stood and walked over to the coffee urn, his face in puzzlement.

As he drew his cup of coffee, his back to her, he said slowly, "All right, but let's take the long view. You're possibly familiar with the reasons Number One felt the war had to be precipitated. It was either that or economic collapse on the part of Alphaland, the strongest power on this planet. What follows such a collapse, Till? How many of the neutral economies are tied in with that of Alphaland, how many currencies backed by the gold Alpha?"

He turned and faced her when his cup was full. "Take the long view. Suppose you attain your goal. Alphaland's economy collapses. What will we have left, a vacuum for the Karlists to fill?"

A voice from the door said, "What's wrong with the Karlists?"

Ross turned his head. It was a roly-poly man in the robes of a Temple Monk.

"Pater Riggin," Tilly exclaimed in welcome.

XI

"Is THAT COFFEE?" the Temple Monk asked, making his way to the urn.

Combs stood there, cup in hand, scowling at the newcomer. He made no motion to get out of the way.

Most of the others in the room, those of the guerrillas who were not confined to their bunks, made their way toward the Temple Monk, the larger number grinning.

The newcomer looked at Centurion Combs slyly. "I suspect, my son, that you have little respect for my cloth."

Combs said ungraciously, "Very little."

The Temple Monk looked about the mess table, noted that there were no clean cups and took up a dirty one. He began to fill it, saying, "Then that makes two of us, eh?"

"What was that?"

"Ummm. Haven't you ever heard the old saying that the more one knows of one's religion, the less one believes?"

Combs was, on the face of it, taken aback. He stuttered indignantly. "If you're saying what I think you're saying, then why not get out of that costume you're wearing?"

The older man laughed at him. "My dear boy, look who's talking. Your own costume isn't exactly the uniform of the country you serve, is it?"

"I'm a guerrilla!"

Pater Riggin raised shaggy eyebrows. Then gesturing with his full cup at them all, said, "And so, I suppose, in a way, am I."

Tilly had come up smiling and had stood silently thus far on the sidelines of the discussion.

She said to Combs, "Knock it, sour-puss. Boys, meet the longest-time guerrilla of us all." She twisted her mouth in her mocking moue. "The espionage agent, the saboteur, the underground operative to shame the most competent."

In his few years in the Central Comita, Ross Westley had seen Pater Riggin on a few occasions, and even exchanged amenities with him, but although the Temple Monk was well whispered about in innermost party circles, he had never come to know the man more than in passing. The alter ego of Number One; the man behind the throne; the Svengali to the Presidor's Trilby; the only friend before whom the dictator let down his hair. All this he had heard Pater Riggin called, but he had found no evidence to back the charges.

But now this. The Temple Monk in the camp of the enemy, and obviously well-known to some, welcome by all, save possibly the junior officer Combs, a surly one at best.

119

Ross said, "What in the name of the Holy Ultimate are you doing here?"

Pater Riggin, his cup in his left hand, patted his tummy with his right, like nothing so much as a jovial Santa Claus. "I might ask you the same, Coaid Deputy."

Tilly said, "I'm afraid that handle no longer quite fits Rossie. We had to pull a cloak and dagger rescue."

Ross, still confused, snapped, "I am not so sure it was a rescue. When my hearing came up, I would have had my say."

The one called Altshuler laughed lowly.

Tilly tilted her head and looked up at the deposed propaganda head. "Rossie, Rossie. There was to be no hearing. You were on your way to be shot."

A chill went through him, but he demanded, "How do you know?"

Most of those present, now crowded around the table, laughed. They seemed to do a great deal of laughing and joking, Ross realized impatiently. Was it a characteristic of those continually in extreme danger? A bravado brought on by the proximity of death?

Tilly said, mocking, "How did we know where you were and that you'd be passing that exact spot where we picked you away from Fielder's Surety men, lover-mine? Let me give you an idea of just how well we are worked into the fabric of Alphaland. It was Jet Pirincin, who sits immediately outside your private offices, who smelled a rat when she saw you leave with the Temple Bishop. She relayed the message. So we got in contact with one of our other inside people, in Surety, who was able to get the details of what was to happen to you, and where. So, deciding that even though Alphaland might think you expendable, Betastan didn't, we jumped on our horses and dashed off in all directions to the rescue."

Ross was staring at her.

"You mean to tell me that Jet Pirincin is a Betastani agent? And that you also have them planted in the other commissariats in such Surety spots?"

"Certainly not," she said.

"Then what do you mean?"

"Jet Pirincin, my dear Rossie, is a most patriotic citizen of Alphaland. She—"

He interrupted her, blurting, "You don't make any sense at all!"

"She's a Karlist."

He held a long silence, then finally turned to look at Pater Riggin who had been beaming away, all the while sipping his coffee.

"And so are you!" Ross accused.

The Temple Monk nodded.

Ross turned on Tilly, then shot his eyes to Combs and around at the others. Most of them were grinning and eying him expectantly, though he couldn't think why that should be in their expressions.

· It came to his lips before it was fully comprehended in his mind. "So are the rest of you!"

The Temple Monk put down his empty cup. He sighed and said, "Let us be seated. I am sure we've all been through a great deal in the past hours. However, there is no opportunity for much rest, and we're even short of time for explanation."

He took his own advice and utilized one of the benches that ran along the mess table. Six or eight of the others, including Ross, Tilly and Combs, seated themselves as well, but the others remained standing.

Pater Riggin brought his eyes back to Ross and said, "My son, you do not suppress an ideal by butchering its adherents, unless you are in position to liquidate them all. Even then it may germinate among others. This most certainly applies to social systems. Decimate the adherents enough and they will go underground, perhaps, but the teachings remain—be they right or wrong—and

121

will hibernate until opportunity presents itself again to make a bid for realization."

"Then in spite of Number One's efforts for the past half century, the Karlist movement remained in existence, underground?" Ross asked.

"Correct."

Ross looked at Tilly, scowling. "But what's this got to do with the extent to which you Betastani have infiltrated Alphaland?"

"Dom't be dense, Rossie. Had we been limited to signing up Alphaland traitors and buying the money-hungry, we would have had a small underground indeed. But when we were able to gain the cooperation of a whole socioeconomic movement, comparatively small though its membership might be, we had on our side an organization of dedicated idealists. And that you can't beat when you're in the clutch, Rossie mine."

"Then you're all, all damned Karlists!" he snapped.

Pater Riggin put back his rounded head and laughed.

"My son, my son. Please remember that I lived through the civil war, heard the slogans, even helped write the diatribes against the movement. Sat at the side when the leaders, some of whom were long-time friends, were tried and shot. Participated through it all as an active anti-Karlist."

"But you just said . . ."

The older man held up a hand. "To my shame and sorrow, it was not until later that I was able to rise above the slogan level and actually investigate the teachings of these people. It was then that I became converted—much too late to have got myself shot as an adherent."

Ross was scowling at the Temple Monk. From the side of his eyes, he could see Tilly Trice watching him intently with an element of worry there. This was apparently of the greatest importance to Tilly. He refused to consider the obvious reason why.

Pater Riggin was more serious now.

"Ross Westley, most great beliefs, ideals, can be summed up in a sentence or two. If they need more, then there is a weakness, the belief is not whole. So then, in your own words, tell me what you think the basic teaching of the Karlists is?"

Ross looked at him. All his life, since he had been a child at the knee of the passionate Franklin Westley, he had been subjected to the anti-Karlist teachings. In these, his later years, he had even participated in spreading them. Long, supposedly, after the Karlists had been a danger.

Anti-Karlism was a dogma, a faith, he knew. Decades past, the adherents of Number One had dug out every last book or pamphlet written by that organization's leaders and had burned them. Every novel, ever so lightly tinged, every play, or even verse, that could be accused of Karlist leanings—all were destroyed. It came to him now that he, Deputy of Information, had never actually read a true Karlist book or article. Oh yes, books on socioeconomics which had quoted in limited amounts from this work or that, the better to criticize and condemn the movement, but the basic works of the enemy? He didn't know, but he doubted if even Number One had them in his private library. Or even Mark Fielder.

His voice, as though in spite of himself, was wild again. "They're anarchists. They want to tear down everything that their betters have built. They want to turn society on its head and let the yokes rule their superiors."

Altschuler said softly, for once without humor, "That, fella, is exactly what we don't want to do. You've been reading your own propaganda again."

Pater Riggin volunteered. "Let me do it for you. In a sentence, Ross Westley, the basic belief of the Karlists is that government should be instituted to help realize the full potentialities of each member of society."

123

Ross was put to staring again.

He shook his head in disgust. "Any government subscribes to that!"

But Pater Riggin shook his head right back. "Then most of them lie. Because most governments are instituted to maintain the privileges of a minority, against the interest of society as a whole. The interest of society as a whole is to realize the full potentialities of each individual member of society."

Ross continued to stare, his indignation waning.

The older man pressed on. "They will all *say* that is their goal, but they lie. A socioeconomic system based on an aristocracy, such as feudalism, keeps at the helm a nobility that is not necessarily competent. Many an emperor or king, down through the ages, was actually insane. I mention in passing such as Caligula and George Third of England."

Ross said, "What's that got to do with the policy of the government being directed at realizing the full potentialities of the people?"

"My son," the Temple Monk said with a twinkle, "if the ultimate head of the government is in a job that has nothing to do with real capabilities and potentialities, what can we expect on lower levels?

"But to go on. Various other socioeconomic systems have been seen in which the possessors of power and wealth dominated government to the benefit of themselves and their immediate relatives and friends. As good an example as any was England during the Nineteenth and Twentieth Centuries of Mother Earth. The British writer, Somerset Maugham, once wrote that he had met many of the top leaders of government and was at first surprised at how indifferently intelligent they were. He came to the conclusion that it didn't take particularly intelligent people to run a government. Of course, finally, under the administrations of these incompetents, Great Britain became a third-rate power.

"To go on still further, we find the so-called communists of the Twentieth Century. Rip-snorting idealists when first they came to the helm, we were soon able to observe that party membership and relationship to ranking members of the hierarchy counted most when it came to obtaining high office. Ability was not necessarily the thing. The son of Stalin, although known as a problem drinker, quickly became a general of the air force; the son-in-law of Khrushchev was soon top editor of *Pravda*."

The Temple Monk was smiling at him. "I submit, Ross Westley, that none of these socioeconomic systems was in truth utilizing the full potentialities of the citizenry. If at the top you do not have the most suited elements guiding the country, certainly all the way down the line nepotism, the power of money, and a score of other factors will hinder many from realizing their most.

"Do you know the real motivation of Number One and his Old Hands when they fought the Karlists in the streets? Whatever the highblown slogans they repeated ad nauseam, in actuality they were fighting to preserve a system of privilege. Your father was fighting to preserve a system under which he could hand down his high office to you, his beloved son, in spite of the fact that you were unsuited to hold it. He must have known it, toward the end of his life, but that didn't prevent him from urging Number One to appoint you to the position. I suspect you do not even like the job as Propaganda Deputy, but so it is. You, though one of the highest ranking officials in Alphaland, would be more suited to be a professor of history, and undoubtedly happier. I suspect Emperor Caligula would have been better off had he lived under a system where he would have found his own level, based on his true abilities, rather than having been born into the Julian family and being shunted into the Imperium."

The historian in Ross Westley prevented him from being at sea in this. He said slowly, "Perhaps the stated

125

purpose of your organization is very fine, however, I wonder to what extent government is needed for a man to realize his true worth, under any society. Top men will come to the top under any socioeconomic system."

Altshuler leaned forward. "Are you sure? Or are you confusing the fact that the men in control will proclaim that they are top men? Gangsters such as Stalin, Hitler, Mussolini, Chiang Kai-shek and Franco, to name a handful at one period in history, will shoot their way to power, and then, the propaganda machine in their hands, the schools, entertainment and news media in their hands, will proclaim themselves the top elements of the country, the best and most intelligent. Who in Nazi Germany wasn't led to believe that those who led were the best, most idealistic and dedicated men in the land?"

Pater Riggin took over again.

"Admittedly, some men, of certain types, will struggle to the top given any society. However, many of our most capable are not of this nature. For instance, the early American electrical wizard, Steinmetz, was a cripple. Had he been born a slave in Roman society, he would have been knocked over the head at birth, his potentialities never realized. Some of our artists, poets and such, are not of the caliber to fight. It is no coincidence that the three great poets of the British romantic period, Byron, Shelley and Keats, were all protected from want throughout their lives. Byron was a lord, Shelley a baron, Keats from a well-to-do family. But suppose any of them had been born into a life of child labor in the mills of Manchester? Would any of them have become poets? Their contemporaries, such as Leigh Hunt and Thomas Hood, born into poverty, were possibly their equals in talent, but had to spend their lives doing newspaper work, writing reviews, or humorous verse meant for the semi-literate."

Ross said, suddenly impatient, "All right, this could

go on forever. The point is, you admit that you're subversives."

Combs said curtly, "Proud of it."

Pater Riggin said, "It's all according to what you're subverting, Ross Westley, whether or not the term is a derogatory one. Jesus was a subversive, and so were Washington and his coaids."

Feeling irritation at being on the defensive, Ross struck out. "You tell a fine story, *Pater* but to reinforce Centurion Combs' opinion when you first entered, let me point out that you yourself wear a garb that doesn't exactly proclaim you a liberal. You mentioned Washington, did you ever run into this quotation from a coaid of his, Thomas Jefferson? 'In every country and in every age, the priest has been hostile to liberty. He is always in alliance with the despot, abetting his abuses in return for protection of his own.'"

Even as he quoted, the words of Temple Bishop Stockwater about the lesson of Mexico came back to him and he finished by saying slowly, "I am afraid your United Temple sees the handwriting on the wall this time and is attempting to repair its public image."

"Too late," Altshuler grinned. "The ball's already begun to bounce."

Ross looked at the subversive Temple Monk again. "You haven't explained remaining in the United Temple."

Pater Riggin shrugged his fat padded shoulders. "For one thing, it was the perfect protective covering. But there's another thing, Ross." His face lost its humor. "A people get the religion they want and deserve, just as they get the government they want and deserve, on an average and given time. A false religion remains a popular one only so long as the people support it; an antiquated socioeconomic system remains only so long as the people support it."

His chuckle now was sour. "When the majority of the

people on this planet no longer accept belief in the Holy Ultimate and the United Temple, which represents this conception, then it will wither away. Not before. Attacking the organization physically might drive it underground, but never destroy it. It will be destroyed only by education and man's evolution to a higher level of understanding."

Tilly, who had remained uncharacteristically silent, spoke up. "Rossie," she said, the old mockery in the back of her words, "you're desperately fighting your friends and I suspect that inwardly you know it."

"What's that supposed to mean, Till?" he snapped angrily.

"I think you know. Individuals, no matter of how much goodwill, are apathetic when it comes to changes in the institutions with which they are familiar. They will put up with almost anything before facing the need of changing basic cultural habits, political forms, religions or socioeconomic systems. For instance, I suspect that in actuality you believe the United Temple to be parasitical. But all your life you have paid it lip service, and I suspect too, in argument about the desirability of maintaining the institution, you would drag up some moth-eaten opinion supporting the need for keeping the ignorant happy, or teaching the basic virtues, or some such. You've been dragging your heels about speaking up and announcing what you truly believe."

He looked at her unhappily.

Altshuler laughed. "Tilly, you sound like a soapbox lecturer, rather than the head of a couple dozen ragged guerrillas."

She snorted back at him. "One's as important as the other, each in its place."

She came to Ross again. "The same apathy applies in the field of political economy. Look back over your history, Rossie, and consider how long some people put up with ridiculous social systems after everyone in the nation, for all practical purposes, knew them to be ridiculous.

"But that apathy, given a spark, can be changed overnight to the desire for changes. Had you suggested, one year before the Declaration of Independence, that complete freedom from England was the only solution to the problems of the colonists, you probably would have been stoned in the streets. Lenin wrote, less than six months before coming to power, that he never expected to live long enough to see the proletarian revolution. And so it goes.

"Rossie, the Karlists have been waiting a long time for this opportune moment. The Alphaland invasion of Betastan was the spark that set things underway. Not only in Alphaland, where your people are already on the streets in revolt against the war and the government of Number One and his Coaids, but in Betastan as well."

Gonzales, the electronics expert, spoke up for the first time. "And in four or five of the neutrals, according to radio. Karlists in some of those countries were kept from acting, only because they were afraid of the Alphaland air marines intervening if they tried anything, but with this country tied up, the revolt was on."

Tilly's voice went persuasive. "What does it take to bring you around, lover-mine? In your secret heart you've known for a long time where you really stood. Otherwise you wouldn't have been leaking information to me that could be used against Number One."

Ross looked from her to Pater Riggin, to Combs, to Altshuler, to Bernal and the rest. And then, desperately, completely around the circle again.

He stood suddenly. "What do you expect from me?" he demanded.

"Sit down, son," Pater Riggin said mildly. "We'll bring you up to date."

He pursed his plump lips. "In actuality, there has been as much unscheduled change in Betastan as there has been here. At present, real government is in the hands of the guerrillas, the leaders of whom are Karlists. They wish as quick an end of hostilities as possible so that they can present their program to the people for an immediate vote."

"And what is their program?"

"Immediate amalgamation with Alphaland, with the eventual aim of world government."

"WHAT!"

The false Temple Monk looked at him without answer.

Ross blurted, "But that's Number One's program!"

Tilly tinkled laughter. The young guerrillas around her chuckled softly.

Pater Riggin said slowly, "Only to a certain point, Ross. To a certain point it is the program of any thinking person. This planet is well suited for a unified government and has been for some time; Betastan and Alphaland being so delicately balanced has stood in the way of such a unification. Number One, of course, has wished world rule—under Number One and his Coaids. That is rejected, obviously, by the Karlists. The new government will be decided upon by representatives from all the participating countries—a Constitutional Convention, you might call it, with the basic theory of the Karlists behind it."

Ross slumped back in his seat.

For the moment they didn't disturb him, though watching carefully, waiting for a response that they all seemed to expect. All, perhaps, except Centurion Combs who had a cynical expression on his youthful face.

Ross Westley finally took a deep breath and said, "All right. What has all this got to do with me? What is it you want from me?"

A sigh went through them.

Two or three of the exhausted irregulars, as though

this were all that had been keeping them from needed rest, went back to their bunks.

Pater Riggin quickly outlined the developments of the past twenty-four hours, during which time Ross had been recovering from his concussion.

"Fielder and his triumvirate are making their bid for power. They won't win, eventually, but unless thwarted now, they'll cause endless additional bloodshed."

"What can we possibly do to prevent them?"

The former Temple Monk said, "A great deal. The strongest positions they hold are Surety, the military and Finance, none of which are particularly popular now for obvious reasons."

"Well," Ross said sarcastically. "We hold nothing."

Pater Riggin arched his eyebrows. "To the contrary, we have Number One, himself, you, the Deputy of Information, and Philip McGivern, head of the Department of Socioeconomics though he is now hospitalized."

Ross looked at the older man as though he were mad. "You expect Number One to support a Karlist take-over?"

The other smiled and shook his heavy head. "Not exactly. I expect him to combat a take-over by Fielder, Croft-Gordon and Matheison. In his present fury—I might mention, he is not a particularly intelligent man —he is not taking the long view. He would rather pull his whole world down around his shoulders, than see his immediate enemies prevail over *him*. It is a characteristic of dictators, so I understand."

Ross thought about it briefly.

"Well," he said. "You've got your work cut out. Let's say that we could write up a speech for Number One to give. It would call upon everyone to put down their arms and support the movement for a democratic conference to plan a world government. He would resign his office, as a gesture of sincerity, call upon Alphaland forces to return to their homeland immediately. I could give another, brief talk to back him. So could Academecian McGivern. But there's one bug in the ointment."

Tilly and Pater Riggin looked at him.

"And what is that?"

"They have the communications system in their control, not us."

Tilly yawned mightily and came to her feet. "That's where we come in. Combs! Altshuler! Bernal! Come on, fellas, all of you. On your feet. Gonzales, put out a general alarm to all our groups. Project Propaganda goes into effect."

The men in the bunks groaned.

One yelled over, "Why didn't you characters keep on talking? It was like being rocked to sleep."

Gonzales headed for the electronics equipment in the corner, and Ross, looking after him, wondered what complicated Rube Goldberg devices they could have dreamed up to avoid detection by Mark Fielder's Surety.

He turned to Tilly and said, "How many men can you gather?"

Tilly thought about it, twisting her mouth. "'Bout five hundred to a thousand, as of this morning. Maybe some of them have been killed or taken since then."

Pater Riggin said, "We've got to get working on that speech. Wait for me here. I'll have to check with Jim. He'll be boiling, I've been gone so long from where I've got him stashed out."

"Who's Jim?" Combs growled.

Pater Riggin looked at him. "Number One."

Combs grunted. "It never occurred to me the cloddy had a first name."

Pater Riggin murmured, "Everybody has a first name —to the right person." He added softly. "It's been a task remaining that right person for so many years, waiting for this moment." He was gone.

The room was a bedlam as men sought their weapons and other equipment.

Ross and Tilly Trice stood alone, momentarily, looking into each other's faces.

"And when it's all over?" he said.

"Like I said," she told him.

It all hit him at once. He said in pure astonishment, "But you people have won. And you haven't had the use of a single computer to figure it out."

She grinned at him mockingly.

"Oh, I've had a computer. So've we all."

He scowled at her, uncomprehendingly.

She tapped her head.